It's a Picnic!

Nancy Fair McIntyre

It's a Picnic!

ILLUSTRATED BY ABNER GRABOFF

A WILLIAM COLE BOOK

NEW YORK / THE VIKING PRESS

To Bill and Megan for all the joyous
picnics we have shared

Contents

Introduction

Here's a world of picnics for every occasion under the sun — from grandstand snacks to country banquets. Mix or match them as you like; for the most part they are interchangeable. The soup that goes to the game also goes to sea; the dish that's fit for a country banquet also brightens a fantail party. All recipes in this book are planned for six; multiply or divide them according to your needs.

Picnics today vary from the classic feasts of the nineteenth century. Who can forget Little Red Riding Hood's picnic basket for Grannie: "one dozen brown hen's eggs, a jar of honey, a pound of butter, a bottle of elderberry wine, and a screw of snuff"?

Watteau and Manet painted the Sybaritic, sun-dappled delights of the outdoor banquet. Medieval court tapestries and ancient Chinese scrolls record its venerable heritage. While the movable feast has been eulogized, painted, and savored for centuries, it took the French to give it a name. *Piquenique* — as it was originally called in 1692 — means to "pick up a trifle."

Trifle or banquet, modern picnics aren't confined to Elysian settings or prescribed ritual. They pack up and follow the action. A picnic is a thermos of warming soup in a duck blind at dawn, a motel breakfast out of a hamper, or a hearty casserole from the galley. With thermal equipment to keep foods hot or cold for hours, the picnic travels with greater style and convenience than ever before. Picnicking has never been more inviting, easier, or less restrictive.

Be as elaborate or simple as you want, but please don't limit the menu to routine foods or delicatessen shortcuts. A good picnic is a respite from the ordinary, an escape from routine, a time for adventurous feasting. Even such familiar picnic classics as fried chicken and potato salad arrive in style if prepared with a little imagination and added seasonings.

My husband and I discovered the joys of picnicking in Italy, especially on the trains, in third class, but it was not until we moved to Laguna Beach, California, with its year-round chamber-of-commerce climate that we became impassioned picnickers. This area of Riviera-style coastline where we live, halfway between Los Angeles and San Diego, is a picnic paradise — from the sandy coves of Laguna to the camper sites near Palm Springs, from the hiker trails of the mountains to the back-country meadows where banquets in a basket unfold under a live-oak tree.

Here's to the picnic — one of the last blissful, individual joys of man not yet computerized, psychoanalyzed, or taxed!

It's a Picnic!

CHAPTER I

Picnic Classics

The old-fashioned family picnic is a sentimental repast that every American knows by heart from the deviled eggs to the watermelon. This familial feast has sparked some great picnic classics — foods that typify the wholesome charm of the American kitchen. While the cooking is traditional, it need not be routine or unimaginative. The homespun picnic won its acclaim on specialties that were the equal of any epicurean dish.

Today, alas, the majority of old-fashioned picnics are straight from the little old supermarket. Despite what the label proclaims, "Grannie's Old-Time Products" can't compete with your own freshly made salads and meats. Homespun picnics must be homespun.

The time and effort involved in preparing a hamperful of treats are well repaid by the salute you'll receive from your troops, for a family still travels on its stomach. The better the food, the happier the outing. Whatever you make, make it festive and interesting — not just the same-old-

3

cole-slaw but the zestiest cole slaw, the tastiest hamburger, the most succulent ham.

Give this picnic the affectionate preparation it deserves. It's just as important as any other picnic — maybe more so.

Real "Real Southern Fried Chicken"

Queen of the picnic classics is southern fried chicken. The following recipe I inveigled from a gentleman from Louisiana who claims that it is the *real* "real southern fried chicken" as prepared at home on the mortgaged plantation. It's like nothing you've ever tasted in Dixie restaurants, we promise.

2 fryers, cut in serving pieces	2 eggs, beaten
2 cups flour seasoned with salt and pepper	1 tsp oregano
	1 tsp rosemary
4 cups cooking oil	1 tsp tarragon
salt to taste	1 tsp paprika
MARINADE	2 cloves garlic, crushed
2 cups cooking oil	

Wash and dry the chicken pieces and place in a shallow pan. Combine the ingredients for the marinade and pour marinade over chicken, turning pieces to coat them on both sides. Let marinate about 2 hours, then remove chicken from pan and dip the individual pieces in the seasoned flour. Since you'll need two large skillets to cook the chicken, pour 2 cups cooking oil in each skillet and heat oil until it is hot enough to sizzle when tested with a drop of water. Brown the chicken pieces quickly on all sides. When all are golden brown, cover pans, reduce heat, and cook *slowly* until chicken is tender, about another 20 minutes. Salt the chicken generously as you fry it; poultry absorbs a lot of salt.

Potato Salad De Luxe

Commercial packaging has demoted the potato salad to the rank of potato third class. Too bad, for it is a marvelous salad when prepared with a little imagination.

8 medium-sized new potatoes	4 hard-cooked eggs, diced
1 can bouillon	chopped parsley
1 large red onion, chopped finely	salt and pepper
12 cherry tomatoes	1 cup homemade mayonnaise (see following recipe)
1 4-oz can artichoke hearts, drained and sliced	

Boil the potatoes in their jackets until tender. Drain, cool, peel, and slice. Marinate them in the bouillon for an hour. Put chopped onion into a salad bowl with the whole cherry tomatoes, sliced artichoke hearts, diced hard-cooked eggs, and a sprinkling of chopped parsley. Add salt and pepper to taste. Just before packing the salad, drain the potatoes from the marinade, add, and stir in the mayonnaise.

Homemade Mayonnaise

The difference homemade mayonnaise makes in potato salad, or anywhere mayonnaise is used, is spectacular. So why not be spectacular — especially when you can whip up mayonnaise so effortlessly with an electric beater? This one, made with salad oil, is lighter than mayonnaise with an olive-oil base.

1 cup salad oil	3 Tbsp lemon juice or white vinegar
2 eggs	
$\frac{1}{2}$ tsp dry mustard	$\frac{1}{4}$ cup salad oil
$\frac{3}{4}$ tsp salt	

Measure 1 cup salad oil and set aside. Break the eggs into a mixing bowl, add the dry mustard, salt, lemon juice or white vinegar, and the ¼ cup salad oil. Turn on electric beater at slowest speed and blend these a few seconds. Now pour in the 1 cup of salad oil in a steady stream, taking not more than 15 seconds blending time from start to finish. Turn electric beater on high speed for 5 seconds more. Behold! Fresh mayonnaise! Makes 1¼ cups.

Stuffed Eggs —Two Ways

To forget the stuffed eggs on a classic picnic is an unspeakable crime. They're a sentimental tradition. There's no tradition, however, on *how* to stuff an egg. Be as versatile as you like and invent your own stuffing or try one of these.

Deviled Crab Stuffing

12 **hard-cooked eggs**
½ **cup boned, flaked crab-meat**
2 **tsp Parmesan cheese**
3 **Tbsp butter**
2 **Tbsp mayonnaise**

1 **tsp Worcestershire sauce**
2 **Tbsp minced chives**
2 **Tbsp minced parsley**
¼ **tsp Tabasco sauce**
salt and pepper to taste

It's an art to hard-cook an egg so it is firm but not tough. The secret lies in cooking *slowly*. Be sure to have the eggs at room temperature; if they're cold they will crack in hot water. Bring a pan of water to below the simmering point (the French call this "smiling water"). Gently put in the eggs. Cook them slowly for 15 minutes. Remove the eggs and cover them immediately with cold water. Let them cool before peeling them.

Cut the eggs in half and remove yolks. Mix together the

flaked crabmeat, Parmesan cheese, butter, mayonnaise, Worcestershire sauce, minced chives, parsley, and Tabasco sauce. Salt and pepper to taste. Mash the egg yolks and add to mixture. Blend well and spoon into egg-white cavities.

Mushroom Stuffing

12 hard-cooked eggs
12 fresh mushrooms
2 Tbsp green chopped onions
2 tsp chopped parsley

2 Tbsp butter
2 Tbsp dry sherry
salt and pepper to taste

Cook and peel 12 eggs as in preceding directions. Cut them in half and remove yolks. Chop the fresh mushrooms, add chopped green onions and parsley. Melt the butter in a saucepan and add the mushroom mixture, dry sherry, and salt and pepper to taste. Sauté a few minutes. Blend with mashed egg yolks and fill egg cavities. Chill in refrigerator.

Hot Dog!

From Coney Island's Red Hots to California's foot-long Doggies, the hot dog reigns unchallenged as America's favorite sandwich. Grilled plain or embellished with a sauce, there's nothing quite like a hot dog, except another hot dog — who can eat only one? Here are two ways to cook them. Buy the best quality, please!

Cheese-Bacon Hot Dogs

6 frankfurters
6 wedges cheddar cheese

6 slices uncooked bacon
6 toothpicks

Split the frankfurters and insert a wedge of cheddar cheese in each. Wrap each with a slice of uncooked bacon and anchor with a toothpick. Wrap individually in aluminum foil, cheese side down, leaving the top open. Grill over coals 7 or 8 minutes, or until bacon is done.

Barbecued Hot Dogs

Marinate the hot dogs in this lively barbecue sauce and also use it for basting as you grill.

6 **frankfurters**	1 **tsp paprika**
¼ **cup chopped onions**	6 **Tbsp chili sauce**
2 **Tbsp salad oil**	6 **Tbsp water**
2 **tsp brown sugar**	3 **Tbsp vinegar**
1 **tsp dry mustard**	1 **Tbsp Worcestershire sauce**
½ **tsp salt**	**dash Tabasco**
½ **tsp pepper**	

Sauté the onions in the salad oil. Add all the rest of the ingredients and simmer for 15 minutes. Score the frankfurters and marinate them in the sauce a couple of hours.

P.S. Did you know that hot dogs are great with horseradish or Taco sauce?

Burgers

Ham is the only thing a hamburger doesn't have. It's been combined with everything else you can think of — cheese, fruit, peanut butter, vegetables, nuts, and a wild variety of spices. This is the custom-built sandwich tailored to your own taste — and anything goes! Put it on French bread, onion rolls, rye toast, or bagel; dress it up or dress it down; grill it, fry it, broil it; have it rare or well done, hot or cold — it's still the beloved burger and practically indestructible. (Except by those burger stands which dispense mass-produced hamburgers that are half filler and thin as a pancake — a burger has to have at least ¼ lb meat to be worthy of its name.) However you build your burger, you might like to try some new combinations. Here are three of my favorites.

Walnut-Cheese Burgers

1½ lb ground round steak (or sirloin, if you are feeling expansive)
1 Tbsp Worcestershire sauce
1½ tsp salt
½ tsp pepper
2 Tbsp ice water
1 cup grated cheddar cheese
½ cup chopped walnuts

Combine the meat with Worcestershire sauce, salt, pepper, and ice water. Mix lightly with a fork and add the grated cheese and chopped walnuts. Shape into 6 patties (¼ lb each), but don't pack down the meat with a heavy hand. Hamburger should be loose or "fluffy" enough to breathe. Grill to desired color — pink is the best.

Mozzarella Burgers

1½ lb ground round steak
2 Tbsp ice water
1½ tsp salt
½ tsp basil
½ tsp oregano
½ tsp pepper
¼ cup tomato sauce
6 slices mozzarella cheese

Combine the meat with the ice water, salt, basil, oregano, pepper, and tomato sauce. Blend well and divide meat into 12 patties. Place a slice of mozzarella cheese on each of 6 patties and top with the remaining 6 patties; press edges together. Grill to taste, but long enough for the cheese to melt slightly.

Hawaiian Chutney Burgers

1½ lb ground round steak	2 Tbsp ice water
1½ tsp salt	6 heaping Tbsp chutney
½ tsp pepper	

Combine the meat with the salt, ice water, and pepper. Divide meat into 12 patties and put a heaping Tbsp of chutney in center of 6 patties. Cover with the remaining 6 patties; press edges together. Make the following sauce.

Sauce

¼ cup salad oil	½ tsp ginger
¼ cup soy sauce	1 clove garlic, crushed
2 Tbsp corn syrup	2 green onions, sliced thin
1 Tbsp lemon juice	

Combine all ingredients. Grill the burgers to taste, basting frequently with the sauce.

Piccalilli Relish

It's the little touches that give a picnic heart and warmth. One of these is *fresh* piccalilli to serve with meat, chicken, and particularly hot dogs and hamburgers. If you always thought piccalilli was something that came off the grocer's shelf, wait till you try it fresh from your kitchen!

10 cucumbers, peeled and sliced thin	¾ cup coarse salt
	4½ cups sugar
4 medium-sized green peppers, seeded and sliced thin	1 qt cider vinegar
	2½ Tbsp whole mixed pickling spices
4 medium-sized onions, sliced thin	½ Tbsp celery seed
2½ qts water	½ Tbsp mustard seed

Soak the prepared cucumbers, peppers, and onions for 12 hours in a brine composed of the water and coarse salt. Drain well. In a saucepan, bring to a boil the cider vinegar and sugar. Put into a cheesecloth bag the pickling spices, celery seed, and mustard seed and tie with string. Add this to the vinegar-sugar liquid along with the drained cucumbers, onions, and peppers. Bring again to a boil and remove cheesecloth bag. Cool vegetable-and-vinegar mixture. Pack in sterilized, airtight jars. Makes approximately 3 qts.

Grilled Corn on the Cob

Freshly picked corn on the cob is an Epicurean treat, even though it lacks the social status of such party vegetables as the queenly asparagus. The corncob never appears at a formal dinner, but it does turn up on a picnic — hooray! Try grilling corn over the coals with this cheese topping.

6 ears young sweet corn
¼ lb butter (or more)
salt to taste

½ cup grated cheddar cheese

Remove husks and silk from the ears of corn. Spread the corn with ¼ lb butter or more, salt to taste, and sprinkle with grated cheddar cheese. Double-wrap individual ears in foil paper. Grill 6 to 8 inches from coals, turning ears every 3 to 4 minutes, until corn is roasted and cheese melted, about 15 to 20 minutes.

Orange Ham

Baked ham evokes visions of old-fashioned, down-on-the-farm picnics served on a checked tablecloth under the elms. Ham is a folksy, homespun meat, but it can be glamorized with different sauces. And why not? There's no virtue in meat so simply prepared that it's dull. Here's a ham with homespun sophistication.

1 5-lb processed or canned ham	¼ cup soy sauce
¼ cup butter	¼ cup dry sherry
½ cup orange marmalade	1 tsp ginger
1 cup orange juice	3 tsp lemon juice
2 Tbsp honey	sliced oranges for garnish

Bake ham on a rack, uncovered, in a medium oven (350°). Allow 30 minutes per lb for processed ham, 15 minutes per lb for canned. Meanwhile melt the butter in a saucepan, add the marmalade, orange juice, honey, soy sauce, sherry, and ginger. Bring to a boil, remove from fire, and add the lemon juice. One half-hour before ham is done, take it out of the oven, cut off the rind (if any), and lavishly spread the orange sauce over the ham. Return ham to oven for another half-hour of cooking. When done, it will have a rich glaze. Garnish with orange slices before serving.

Baked Ham with Pecan Glaze

Here is another way of glamorizing a picnic ham. Who can resist anything with pecans in it?

1 5-lb processed or canned ham	1 cup finely ground pecans
2 egg yolks	peach and pineapple slices
1½ cups combined peach and pineapple jam	

Bake ham as in preceding recipe. One half-hour before it is done, mix egg yolks with peach-pineapple jam, and spread over the ham. Dust meat with the finely ground pecans. Finish baking the ham. Garnish with canned peach and pineapple slices.

Bean Pot

This recipe starts with a can opener, which should endear it to millions of housewives. Much as we discourage canned products, the bean has fared better than most foods in the process of commercialization. There are several good brands of Boston baked beans—the dark brown variety — that are almost as good as homemade. When you add a few of your own flavorings they're even tastier.

1-lb-12-oz can Boston baked beans	2 Tbsp brown sugar
⅓ cup dry sherry	1 tsp dry mustard
	1 tsp instant coffee

Open can of beans (an imperative step) and combine with sherry, brown sugar, mustard, instant coffee. Stir to blend flavors. Pour beans into a bean pot (this will imply to your guests that they're homemade; besides, they taste better in a bean pot). Bake in a slow (275°) oven about 40 minutes until beans are bubbling. The wine and coffee impart a rich, nutty flavor—and nobody will guess how you got it. Smile mysteriously and say nothing.

Cole Slaw in Cheese Dressing

Lunch counters have spoiled the reputation of this classic salad. It inevitably arrives on the blue-plate special, sad and soggy, next to the sad and soggy French fries. The only good cole slaw is the one you make. Here's a unique way of making it with a cheese accent.

3 cups shredded cabbage	1 Tbsp minced chives
3 apples, peeled, cored, and cut into strips	2 Tbsp chopped green onions
½ lemon	1 tsp salt
¼ lb blue cheese	½ tsp pepper
1 Tbsp vinegar	1 cup sour cream
3 Tbsp grated American cheese	

Have shredded cabbage ready in a salad bowl. When you prepare the apple strips, sprinkle with lemon juice to prevent discoloration. Crumble the blue cheese; add to it the vinegar, American cheese, chives, green onions, salt, and pepper. Combine with the sour cream and pour over the cabbage and apples. Toss well.

Steak—Four Ways

If chicken is the queen of the picnic classics, steak is the king. This is the most popular and expensive meat in America. Steak is status. Steak is special. It is also good eating, especially when accented with a lively sauce or seasoning (purists will disagree). The only way to please everyone is to serve individual steaks cooked to personal preference—plain or saucy, rare or well done. Each of the following recipes is for 6 club steaks or shell steaks.

Steak au Poivre

One notable way to grill this luxurious beef is with a liberal coating of crushed pepper (which is removed after cooking) and a splash of cognac.

6 club steaks or shell steaks   4 Tbsp cognac, warmed
3 Tbsp black peppercorns   salt to taste

Crush the peppercorns in a mortar with a pestle until coarsely ground. Dry the steaks with a towel. Rub the crushed peppercorns into both sides of the meat with the palm of your hand. Then wrap the steaks in foil to take to the picnic. When ready to cook, grill the steaks to individual taste and remove from grill. Pour warm cognac over them, stand back, and ignite. The flame will burn just a few moments. When it goes out, scrape off excess pepper, season with salt, and you have a steak with a French touch. This meat is usually served with a brown shallot sauce, but you probably will not want to bother with this on a picnic. If the youngsters don't like the cognac flavoring, omit this step in preparing their steaks.

Steak with Tarragon Marinade

4 Tbsp tarragon vinegar	**½ Tbsp dry mustard**
4 Tbsp finely chopped green onions	**1 cup olive oil**
	¾ cup dry red wine
juice of 1 lemon	**1 Tbsp salt**
3 cloves garlic, chopped	**1 tsp pepper**

Combine all ingredients in a flat pan and marinate steaks for several hours. Carry the marinade to the picnic in a jar and use it to baste steaks while grilling.

Steak with Sky Ranch Steak Glaze

12 Tbsp Roquefort or blue cheese	**juice of ½ lemon**
	3 tsp salt
6 Tbsp butter	**2 tsp pepper**
6 Tbsp scraped onion pulp	
2 Tbsp Worcestershire sauce	
several dashes Tabasco sauce (to taste)	

Combine and cream together the cheese, butter, onion pulp, Worcestershire sauce, Tabasco (use enough for a zesty accent), lemon juice, salt, and pepper. Carry steak glaze to picnic in a jar. When steaks are cooked, spread the glaze on both sides and grill 5 seconds longer on each side, just enough to sizzle the cheese-butter mixture.

Steak with Lime Sauce

Lime is a wonderful accent for steak; it brings out the true flavor of the meat.

3 limes   3 cloves garlic, crushed
3 tsp salt   3 Tbsp olive oil

Cut the limes in half and rub the steaks on both sides, squeezing the juice of ½ lime over each steak. Sprinkle the steaks with salt and crushed garlic. Wrap the steaks in foil and carry to the picnic. Just before grilling, baste with olive oil.

Watermelon Boat

Envision this picnic still life: a plump watermelon scooped out and brimming with cool, colorful fruit—golden peaches, bright strawberries, lush pineapple, bananas, grapes. What a happy way to tote a melon to the party and have it serve as a container, too! If you're ambitious enough, melons can be scooped out and the shells cut in various designs, such as baskets. However, if melon art is not your forte, cut about a quarter of the watermelon off the top and scoop out the bottom, making a "boat." Cut the melon meat into balls, with a cutter, and fill the shell with melon balls and all the lovely fruits of the season. Squeeze a lemon over the fruits to prevent discoloration and toss them well. Cover with the top shell, wrap in foil, and leave in the refrigerator until departure. Carry the following light wine dressing in a separate container and mix it with the fruits before serving.

Wine Dressing

¾ cup dry white wine   1 Tbsp lemon juice
1½ Tbsp sugar   ¾ cup salad oil
1½ tsp salt

Combine the ingredients and put in a jar. Chill in refrigerator.

Homemade Peach Ice Cream

Classic picnics close with a sweet sentiment—a dessert as pretty and old-fashioned as a lacy valentine. What else but homemade, honest-to-goodness, *real* ice cream? If you have a small portable home freezer, make the ice cream at home, take out the dasher, and repack with more ice and rock salt. This peach ambrosia will keep till you reach your destination—and hours longer.

1 cup sugar
2 Tbsp flour
1 cup milk
6 fresh peaches

2 Tbsp lemon juice
1 cup heavy cream whipped
until stiff

Combine sugar, flour, and milk in a saucepan; cook and stir until it thickens. Cool. Peel and pit the peaches; chop and mash into a pulp (or use a blender). There will be 2 cups or more of pulp. Add the pulp and lemon juice to the milk-sugar sauce. Fold in the whipped cream. Put this mixture into the freezer can. Follow standard directions for churning ice cream. Makes 2 qt.

Beach Picnics

Beach picnics vary from New England clambakes to California abalone fries. However, they all have one thing in common: everybody is always hungry.

A hamper of snacks, sandwiches, and refreshing cold drinks is essential to stave off famine before the main picnic dinner is served—especially if this is an all-day-at-the-beach function. Don't forget the ice water, a priceless luxury when the closest water fountain is a speck on the horizon of burning sand.

After hours in and out of the surf, there's nothing more

inviting or cheery than a wood or charcoal fire burning down to glowing coals for a cookout. Build your picnic supper around a barbecue. The kids will insist on hot dogs and hamburgers, but vary the menu with other grilled meats, fish, or chicken for the adults.

The more variety, the more fun. Make several salads. Take a pot of beans. Don't forget the stuffed eggs and all the traditional relishes. Whatever you bring, there will be nothing left over—not even the carrot sticks.

All the picnic classics in this chapter are great to take to the shore. However, if you live in a region where seafood is available, try some of the following barbecues. With fresh seafood flown daily all over the country, New England clambakes merrily cook on the sunny shores of California beaches, and Olympia, Washington, oysters are savored in Florida.

Fish Fry

I always thought the fish fry was as staunchly American as Grandma's preserves until I had it in Italy, where they call it *fritto misto* (mixed fry). The Italians throw a squid and a few shrimp into their fry, but essentially it is the same as ours—delicious! For this skillet dish, use any of the following small fish: smelts, perch, trout, or sand dabs.

12 small fish, cleaned	**1 qt cooking oil**
3 eggs, beaten	**salt and pepper to taste**
3 cups breadcrumbs	

Dip cleaned fish in beaten eggs and roll in breadcrumbs. Salt and pepper to taste. Heat the oil in a skillet until quite hot (375°) and deep-fry fish until golden brown, about 3 or 4 minutes on each side. Drain fish on paper towels.

Hush Puppies

What's a fish fry without hush puppies? Only half a fish fry. These corn-meal dumplings really balance the meal. Stir up the batter at home and have the dumplings ready to cook in a separate skillet while you're frying the fish.

1½ cups white corn meal 1 cup flour
1½ cups water 3 tsp baking powder
⅓ cup milk 2 tsp salt
1 Tbsp vegetable oil 1 tsp sugar
2 tsp grated onion 4 cups cooking oil
2 eggs, beaten

Combine the corn meal and water and cook in a saucepan about 6 minutes, stirring until corn meal becomes stiff and dry enough to roll into a ball. Remove from heat and blend in the milk, together with the vegetable oil, grated onion, and beaten eggs. Sift the flour, baking powder, salt, and sugar. Add to batter and stir thoroughly. When you're ready to fry the hush puppies, drop a Tbsp of batter at a time into the hot cooking oil and fry until golden brown, about 7 minutes. Drain on paper towels.

New England or Anywhere Clambake

All you need for this old-fashioned clambake is some old-fashioned fresh seafood—live lobsters and fresh clams. Living in California, we substitute langouste and local clams; however, if you insist on being terribly New England, wherever you live, you can import live Maine lobsters, cherrystones, and steamers. This is a big-kettle clambake and the easiest kind to produce.

3 **dozen cherrystone clams (or local small hard clams)**

3 **dozen steamer clams (again use local clams if you wish)**

3 **1½-lb to 2-lb live Maine lobsters (or langouste)**

1 **lb seaweed, well washed**

1 **qt water**

6 **medium-sized new potatoes in their jackets, parboiled 15 minutes**

6 **ears fresh corn on the cob, husked**

1 **lb butter**

½ **tsp salt**

juice of 1 lemon

Rinse cherrystone and steamer clams and scrub with a stiff brush until they are free of sand. Rinse lobsters and seaweed until clean. If seaweed isn't available, or you don't want to bother cleaning your own, it can often be bought in fish markets. (Soaked corn husks can be substituted for seaweed.) Line the bottom of a large clambake kettle with the seaweed or sufficient corn husks to make a 4-inch layer. Pour in 1 qt water. Bring to a boil. When kettle is steaming, put in the lobsters or langouste. Cover with a layer of seaweed or husks and then add the potatoes (parboiled to ensure that they will be tender by the time the seafood is cooked.) Cover kettle and steam 20 minutes. Add corn, cover, and cook 10 minutes. Add the cherrystone and steamer clams, cover with a layer of seaweed or husks, cover kettle, and steam until clams open—15 minutes or so. Melt the butter, add the salt and lemon juice, and have this ready to serve with the clams and lobsters. It is traditional to eat the clams first and work down to the corn, potatoes, and lobsters. Remember to strain and serve the lovely nectar in the kettle. Most clam-lobster cookers have a faucet in the bottom to pour off juices. (And remember to remove the lobster stomach—the small sac just behind the head.)

Clams or Mussels Marinière

This seafood feast is all the more fun if you round up your own clams or mussels. (But be sure that they are in season, and also good for eating. Mussels, especially, must be plucked with care.) If you are too lazy to forage for these shellfish, buy them at a fish market. Most Italian fish markets carry mussels, which are a great delicacy. Try them.

6 lb steamer clams or small mussels	**3 Tbsp chopped parsley**
2 cups white wine	**½ cup chopped green onions**
	½ lb butter, melted

Rinse the clams or mussels and scrub with a brush until they are completely free of sand. This is work, but it is vital. You need a big kettle with a tight lid for steaming. When the clams or mussels are clean, put them in the kettle and pour in the white wine. Add the chopped parsley and green onions. Cover the kettle and steam about 10 minutes, or until all the clams or mussels are open and ready to serve. Strain the liquor from the bottom of the kettle and serve on the side as a soup drink. Use the melted butter as a dip. By all means, have a loaf of crusty French bread to dunk in the broth; don't insult this beautiful shellfish marinière by using white sandwich bread.

CHAPTER II

Banquets in a Basket

A dinner party is no picnic, especially the morning-after clean-up. But entertaining *can* be a picnic. Pack a banquet in a basket and move your party outdoors. Fun bubbles in the elixir of country air or salty ocean breezes.

Party picnics are grown-up and elegant, with dishes as delectable as anything served on a damask tablecloth. Make them an occasion. Uncork beautiful wines. Use your prettiest picnicware. Take along a folding table and chairs so that your dining will be as comfortable as possible.

These banquets in a basket are built around a central stellar dish complemented by cold marinated vegetables or an unusual salad. If you want to be really grand, you can have several courses, but usually one will suffice, especially with drinks and appetizers beforehand.

For a finale, we prefer a continental dessert—lovely cheeses, crackers, and fresh fruit. These are more appropriate with a sophisticated meal, and nicer with wine, than a sticky sweet. If you insist on a sweet dessert, make it something small such as petit fours, nothing heavy.

One vital addition to this or any picnic is a good bread. Ordinary white sandwich bread can dampen a picnic quicker than a summer shower. Choose a bread, just as you choose a wine, to complement the meal. Serve either French or Italian bread or one of the moist dark ryes or pumpernickels.

The movable banquet is a happy change of pace from the same old dinner party. And look what you can serve!

Lobster Mousse

Envisioning *le grand piquenique* of several courses, let's begin with lobster mousse. This is a show-off dish, which is just what you want. The nice part is that it isn't much work.

2 Tbsp unflavored gelatin	1 Tbsp minced parsley
2 Tbsp sherry	½ tsp marjoram
½ cup hot chicken broth	2 tsp lemon juice
2 eggs, separated	½ cup mayonnaise
¼ cup minced celery	½ cup heavy cream
2 Tbsp minced green onions	
6 1½-oz canned or cooked lobster meat	

Use a blender for this. Pour in the gelatin, sherry, and hot chicken broth. Whirl for 15 seconds and then add the egg yolks, minced celery, minced green onions, lobster meat, parsley, marjoram, lemon juice, and mayonnaise. Whirl another 15 seconds and add the heavy cream. Beat the egg whites until stiff; fold into the blended mixture. Pour into a wet mold and keep thoroughly chilled until you are ready to serve.

Roast Filet of Beef

Follow the Lobster Mousse with the equally elegant Roast Filet of Beef with Béarnaise Sauce. What if it breaks the budget—this is a party picnic!

1 tsp salt
1 whole beef tenderloin (4 to 5 lb), larded
1 clove garlic, sliced

Have the butcher salt the filet and wrap it in a thin coating of suet to keep it moist during cooking. Insert slices of garlic. Put it on a rack in an open pan and cook in a very hot oven (425°) for about 40 to 50 minutes, allowing 10 minutes to the pound. Don't overcook this luxurious meat; it should be rare and pink. Double-wrap in foil and it will keep warm for an hour; but it's delicious at any temperature, as is the accompanying sauce.

Béarnaise Sauce

Here's a Béarnaise Sauce with a *haute cuisine* elegance, and yet it's so simple to make. The blender does most of the work.

3 egg yolks
2 tsp lemon juice
½ tsp salt
¼ lb butter
1 tsp dried tarragon
2 tsp chopped green onions

2 tsp chopped parsley
¼ tsp salt
¼ tsp pepper
3 Tbsp tarragon vinegar
1 Tbsp water

Put the egg yolks in a blender with the lemon juice and salt. Turn blender on and off to mix seasonings and yolks. Melt the butter in a saucepan until very hot but not brown. Turn blender speed to high and pour the hot butter steadily into blender. Blend for 1 minute until the butter thickens the egg yolks. (What you have here is Hollandaise Sauce.) Next, combine in a saucepan the tarragon, green onions, parsley, salt, pepper, tarragon vinegar, and water. Cook down almost to a glaze consistency; this takes only a few minutes. Add the tarragon glaze to the Hollandaise Sauce and you have a Béarnaise Sauce that would cost you a gold nugget in a restaurant.

Tabbouli

The accompanying *pièce de résistance* for the Roast Filet of Beef is Tabbouli. What's that? It's an exotic Middle Eastern bulgur wheat dish that serves as a salad as well as a starch. It's not only different—it's delicious! Bulgur wheat is usually carried in supermarkets, but if you can't find it in yours, try a food speciality shop.

1½ cups bulgur wheat	3 Tbsp chopped green pepper
8 cups boiling water	½ cup lemon juice
1 cup finely chopped parsley	½ cup olive oil
¼ cup minced fresh mint	2 Tbsp salt
½ cup chopped green onions	freshly ground pepper to
2 large tomatoes, peeled and chopped	taste

The bulgur wheat is "cooked" by a traditional and ancient method: put 1½ cups of bulgur wheat in a bowl and pour 8 cups of boiling water over it. Cover and let stand for several hours or until the wheat is tender and fluffy. Put the wheat in a strainer and shake off any excess water. Stir in the parsley, fresh mint, green onions, tomatoes, green pepper, and—last—the lemon juice, olive oil, salt, and freshly ground pepper to taste. Keep chilled until served.

Stuffed Game Hens

These elegant birds will evoke ohs and ahs from your guests. Wait until they bite into the chic stuffing! Can a stuffing be chic? This one is. Roast the game hens at home and wrap them in foil. They'll stay warm for an hour, and anyway, they're equally tempting at room temperature.

6 **Rock Cornish game hens**
½ **lemon**
3 **tsp salt**
2 **tsp pepper**
12 **chicken livers**
3 **Tbsp butter**
6 **medium-sized mushrooms, sliced**

2 **Tbsp butter**
½ **cup chopped ham**
¼ **cup chopped blanched almonds**
¼ **cup melted butter**
¼ **cup dry white wine**
2 **Tbsp red-currant jelly**

Wash the hens in cold water and rub cavities with half a lemon and the salt and pepper. Sauté the chicken livers in the 3 Tbsp butter a few minutes and chop fine. Sauté the mushrooms in the remaining 2 Tbsp of butter and combine the chicken livers and mushrooms with the ham and almonds. Stuff the hens lightly with this dressing; skewer the openings, tie the legs together, and put the birds, breast side up, in a roasting pan. Combine the ¼ cup melted butter with the wine and red-currant jelly and pour over the hens. Baste frequently. Roast in a 350° oven until birds are fork-tender, about 45 minutes to 1 hour.

Cold Broccoli Salad

The stuffed Game Hens are sufficiently rich to need only a marinated cold vegetable as a side dish (especially if you serve lots of crusty French bread). One vegetable that's more dazzling cold than hot is broccoli; try it with this tart lemon dressing.

2½ **lb fresh broccoli**
½ **tsp salt**
2 **hard-cooked eggs**

LEMON DRESSING

½ **cup lemon juice**
¼ **cup salad oil**

½ **tsp paprika**
1 **tsp sugar**
½ **tsp salt**
1 **clove garlic, minced**
2 **Tbsp finely chopped green onions**

Combine the ingredients for the dressing, preferably the day before if possible, to let the flavors blend. Wash the broccoli and remove leaves and tough part of stalks. Cook the broccoli, covered, in a saucepan containing 1 inch water until barely tender—steam it as the Chinese do. (Don't drown any vegetable in quarts of water. And please don't overcook.) Sprinkle with ½ tsp salt. Take the broccoli and dressing to the picnic in separate containers. Just before serving, pour the dressing over the broccoli and top with chopped hard-cooked eggs.

Côte d'Azur Seafood Casserole

Nothing typifies the party picnic dish as well as this sublime fresh seafood casserole. It's original, festive, and delectable.

2 cups white long-grain rice	3 tsp curry powder
¾ lb fresh cooked crabmeat	2 tsp celery seed
¾ lb fresh shrimp, cooked, peeled, and deveined	2 tsp dry mustard
	½ tsp salt
3 medium-sized green apples, peeled and chopped	¼ tsp pepper
	¾ cup sour cream
5 shallots or green onions, chopped	2 cups mayonnaise
	juice of ½ lemon
⅜ cup peanut oil	parsley

Cook the rice in a minimum amount of water so it is firm rather than soft. Drain and chill. Spread it over the bottom of a buttered casserole dish large enough so the rice is about 2 inches deep. Cover this with the crabmeat, and cover the crabmeat with the shrimp. Sauté the green apples and shallots or green onions in the peanut oil until soft. Add the curry powder, celery seed, mustard, salt, and pepper and let the sauce cool. Combine the cooled sauce with the sour cream, mayonnaise, and lemon juice. Spread the dressing thickly over the top of the casserole; add a few sprigs of parsley for color. Keep the casserole refrigerated and carry it to the picnic in an insulated container.

Chinese Chicken Salad

I can't resist including this celestial salad for those persevering cooks who are willing to track down the Chinese ingredients required. Oriental grocery stores have them. Maybe you've had this dish in a Chinese restaurant and wondered how it was made. The waiter will never tell you. This is top secret in Chinatown, so guard it carefully. This salad makes a beautiful and original picnic course—either as a side dish or a main dish.

1 2½-lb broiler-fryer
1 Tbsp salt
1 carrot, chopped
1 onion, coarsely chopped
1 stalk celery, chopped
2 cups peanut oil
½ cup Chinese *sai fun* (bean threads)

3 cups shredded iceberg lettuce
½ cup chopped green onions
1 Tbsp sesame seeds
½ cup chopped Chinese parsley

Place the chicken in a large pot with water to cover. Add the salt, carrot, onion, and celery. Simmer until chicken is tender. Remove chicken from the pot, take off the skin, and cut meat from the bones in ½-inch slivers. Heat the peanut oil and quickly fry chicken slivers until crisp, 1 or 2 minutes. Remove and drain on paper towels. Next, drop the Chinese bean threads into the hot peanut oil, stirring constantly for a few seconds, until the bean threads are crisp but not brown. (They look like thin crisp noodles.) Remove bean threads from oil and combine with the shredded lettuce, green onions, chicken slivers, and sesame seeds. Top with Chinese parsley. Just before serving, add the following dressing.

Sesame-Seed-Oil Dressing

½ tsp sesame-seed oil	1 Tbsp white wine vinegar
3 Tbsp Chinese plum sauce	1 Tbsp salad oil
1 Tbsp sugar	½ tsp dry mustard

Blend all ingredients and mix with Chinese Chicken Salad.

Indonesian Pork Saté

This is an Indonesian version of shish kebab. (Actually it is not a version of any meat but something completely and irresistibly original.) Saté is made with succulent little morsels of pork threaded on skewers, grilled over coals, and basted with a peanut sauce. It is perfect for a hibachi picnic, but not so exotic that it won't cook on an American grill.

2 ½ lb lean, boneless pork (tenderloin if possible)	1 cup chopped green onions
	3 Tbsp lemon juice
1 cup salted peanuts	¼ cup Japanese soy sauce
2 Tbsp coriander seeds	2 Tbsp brown sugar
2 cloves garlic, minced	½ tsp pepper
1 tsp crushed red peppers, or more	½ cup melted butter
	½ cup chicken stock

Get the best pork you can buy; this recipe deserves it. Cut the pork into squares about 1 inch wide. Cut away any fat; the meat *must* be lean. In a blender, combine the peanuts, coriander seeds, garlic, crushed red pepper (the quantity can be increased if you like a hotter accent, as they do in Indonesia), green onions, lemon juice, Japanese soy sauce, brown sugar, and pepper. Blend these ingredients to the consistency of a purée. Finally, mix the melted butter with the chicken stock and add to the peanut purée.

This is both marinade and basting sauce. Pour it over the pork pieces and let stand several hours. Carry the pork and marinade to the picnic site in a large jar. When you are ready to grill, thread the meat on skewers and cook slowly over low coals, basting with the marinade.

Artichoke-Rice Salad

This exquisite salad comes from a fellow picnic-enthusiast who teams it with cold chicken or meat. It has a kiss of curry and is embellished with pimento-stuffed olives. Please try it—it really dresses up a picnic.

1 package chicken-flavored rice mix

4 green onions, sliced thin

½ green pepper, seeded and chopped

12 pimento-stuffed olives, sliced

2 6-oz jars marinated artichoke hearts

¾ tsp curry powder

⅓ cup homemade mayonnaise (or store-bought if you must)

Cook rice as directed on package, omitting the butter. Cool rice in a large bowl. Add the green onions, green pepper, and olives. Drain the artichoke hearts, reserving the marinade, and cut them in half. Combine artichoke marinade with the curry powder and mayonnaise. Add the artichoke hearts to the rice salad and toss with the dressing. Chill until departure. If you prefer a stronger curry accent, feel free to increase the curry powder. Seasoning is personal in all recipes, and no measurement can be given for all tastes.

Cold Scotch Salmon

The fairest salmon in the world swim the rivers of Scotland. A Scottish picnic of cold salmon and a tankard of ale is as blissful as can be imagined. Try to buy the whole fillet of salmon rather than steaks. The presentation is more dazzling; also the fillet is better for poaching.

3-to-4-lb salmon fillet, or 6 salmon steaks
2 onions, chopped
2 carrots, chopped
2 stalks celery with leaves, chopped
¼ cup butter
½ cup dry white wine
¼ cup chopped parsley
2 cloves
1 bay leaf
1 Tbsp salt
6 peppercorns

In a fish poacher (or a pan sufficiently large to poach the salmon), sauté the onions, carrots, and celery in the butter until vegetables are soft. Add the wine, parsley, cloves, bay leaf, salt, and peppercorns; stir and add 2 qts water. Cover and simmer 5 minutes. Uncover and add the salmon. (If you use a fillet, wrap it in cheesecloth before you put it in the pan; it's easier to remove when cooked.) Simmer, covered, 10 minutes, or until fish flakes easily when you test it with a fork. Chill the salmon in the stock, then remove it and wrap it in foil to keep it moist for the picnic. (In Scotland they carry salmon to a picnic wrapped in lettuce leaves and then in wax paper or foil.) Serve with the following Cold Dill Sauce, which provides half the drama of this spectacular dish.

Cold Dill Sauce

1 egg
1 tsp salt
¼ tsp black pepper
½ tsp sugar
1 Tbsp chopped parsley
4 tsp lemon juice
1 Tbsp chives
2 Tbsp fresh chopped dill weed (use dried dill weed if you must)
1½ cups sour cream

Beat the egg until it is light and fluffy. Add the salt, black pepper, sugar, parsley, lemon juice, chives, and dill weed; then beat in the sour cream. Chill in refrigerator. Carry in separate container. Incidentally, this sauce also complements Lobster Mousse (see Index).

Cucumber Mousse

Cold salmon and cucumber are a classic combination — both have a light, lilting, delicate flavor. This Cucumber Mousse proves again that any way you slice it, a cucumber is superb. Try it with meat too. All these recipes are mix-and-match according to your own tastes.

4 cucumbers
1 cup boiling water
2 Tbsp lemon juice
2 tsp Worcestershire sauce
1 tsp salt
½ tsp white pepper

1 cup mayonnaise
2 envelopes unflavored gelatin
water
1 cup heavy cream, whipped

Peel the cucumbers, cut in half, and remove seeds. Blanch about 5 minutes in the boiling water to which the lemon juice has been added. Drain cucumbers and put in a blender. Blend to a pulp. Cool cucumber pulp and add the Worcestershire sauce, salt, white pepper, and mayonnaise. Dissolve the gelatin in 2 Tbsp cold water and 2 Tbsp hot water. Add to cucumber mixture. Whip the cream until stiff and fold into mixture. Pour into a wet mold and chill. Carry the mold in a cooler and unmold mousse just before serving.

Highland Boiled Potatoes

These Scottish potatoes keep their jackets on when they're cold. They're not only sensible but delicious spuds to whisk off to a gala picnic. Serve them at room temperature with the Cold Scotch Salmon.

18 tiny new potatoes, un-
  peeled
2 Tbsp mint leaves

1 cup mayonnaise
1 Tbsp prepared mustard
2 Tbsp chopped chives

Boil the potatoes in a saucepan, with the mint leaves for flavor, until they are tender but still firm, *not* soggy. Drain and let cool to tepid. Mix the mayonnaise with the mustard and coat the potatoes. Sprinkle with chopped chives. It's best to keep the potatoes chilled en route to the picnic, since dishes with mayonnaise spoil easily on a very hot day.

Cold Chicken Vinaigrette

The true basic salad dressing of France is Vinaigrette Sauce, and there is no dressing more flavorful or versatile. It embellishes many picnic dishes — cold artichokes, shrimp, asparagus, beef—but especially chicken. The oil, vinegar, herbs, and seasonings give a cold boiled chicken a party dress.

6 whole chicken breasts
3 qts water
1 onion studded with 2
  cloves
1 carrot, coarsely chopped

1 stalk celery, coarsely
  chopped
1 bay leaf
6 peppercorns
1 Tbsp salt

Put the chicken breasts in a large pot with the water, clove-studded onion, carrot, celery, bay leaf, peppercorns, and salt. Cover pot and bring to a boil. Skim off foam, replace cover, and simmer until chicken is fork tender, about 30 minutes. Remove chicken from pot. Bone the breasts and remove the skin. Cut breasts in half, making 12 pieces of chicken. Wrap in foil. The Vinaigrette Sauce is spooned over the tepid chicken just before serving.

Vinaigrette Sauce

4 Tbsp wine vinegar	½ tsp dry mustard
1 cup olive oil	2 hard-cooked eggs,
½ cup chopped parsley	chopped
1 Tbsp fresh chopped chives	2 tsp salt (or more, if you
1 Tbsp chopped capers	prefer)
1 Tbsp chopped green onion	1 tsp pepper
1 Tbsp chopped sour pickle	

Blend all ingredients and let sauce stand at room temperature for several hours. Take to picnic in separate container.

Stuffed Spanish Tomatoes

Take these cold, stuffed Andalusian tomatoes to your Chicken Vinaigrette banquet. They are just right, in flavor and color, to share a plate with that beautiful dish. Since the tomatoes are stuffed with rice and seasonings, you won't need any other embellishment except a friendly wine and bread.

6 large ripe tomatoes	5 Tbsp chopped green onions
2 tsp salt	3 Tbsp olive oil
1 tsp pepper	1½ cups firm cooked rice
¼ cup chopped green	about ½ cup mayonnaise
pepper	pimento strips for garnish

Cut tops off tomatoes and scoop out centers. Sprinkle shells with the salt and pepper and turn upside down to drain. Sauté the green pepper and green onions in the olive oil until soft. Combine with the rice. Add ½ cup mayonnaise, or less, depending on taste, and fill tomato cavities with the mixture. Garnish the top with pimento strips and chill until departure. These tomatoes are best carried tightly packed in a plastic container.

Stuffed Artichokes with Shrimp

Stuff an artichoke and you have a dish that is a vegetable, an entrée, and a conversation piece! Here is one that holds a gala seafood salad. Take the artichokes and salad to the picnic separately and fill the artichokes just before serving.

6 **boiled chilled artichokes**	½ **cup mayonnaise**
3 **cups fresh, cooked tiny shrimp (or canned shrimp)**	½ **cup sour cream**
	1 **tsp dill weed**
	1 **Tbsp finely chopped parsley**
3 **green onions, chopped**	
3 **hard-cooked eggs, chopped**	½ **tsp salt**

To prepare artichokes for stuffing, soak them in cold, salted water for 30 minutes. Cut off the stems and pull off the outside bottom row of leaves. Cook artichokes in 1½ inches of water for 45 minutes, or until tender. Gently push aside the center leaves and remove the undeveloped leaves at the heart. With a spoon remove the feathery choke in the center. Leave the succulent artichoke bottom intact. In a bowl, combine the shrimp, green onions, hard-cooked eggs, mayonnaise, sour cream, dill weed, parsley, and salt. Just before serving, stuff each artichoke with approximately ½ cup of this salad.

Beef Vinaigrette

That staunch favorite of the Sunday dinner table, roast beef, takes on new glamour when marinated in this Vinaigrette Sauce. It is similar to the dressing for Cold Chicken Vinaigrette (see Index) but includes a few more spices and a zesty dash of Tabasco sauce.

2 red onions, cut in rings
$\frac{1}{4}$ cup wine vinegar
$\frac{3}{4}$ cup olive oil
4 Tbsp capers
2 Tbsp chopped parsley
2 tsp tarragon
2 tsp chopped chervil
2 tsp chopped chives

2 tsp dry mustard
several dashes Tabasco sauce
2 tsp salt
1 tsp ground pepper
4 cups julienne strips of cooked roast beef (rare beef is best)

Combine all ingredients except the beef. Add the beef strips and marinate 3 or 4 hours. Chill before serving. Serve with a little of the marinade spooned over meat.

Tailgate Picnics

The tailgate picnic epitomizes the fun and freedom of the movable feast. It unfolds wherever you park, country lane or near the stadium. Served buffet-style, it's the easiest of all picnics to stage. Pre-theater picnics from the tailgate buffet are popular from Stratford, Connecticut, to the Hollywood Bowl.

Vitello Tonnato

This is a specialty of Milan, where it is frequently served in outdoor restaurants before an evening at La Scala.

$4\frac{1}{2}$-lb leg of baby veal, boned, rolled, and tied
1 large onion studded with cloves
1 carrot, chopped
1 clove garlic, minced
1 Tbsp salt

1 stalk celery, chopped
$\frac{1}{2}$ tsp rosemary
$\frac{1}{2}$ tsp thyme
$\frac{1}{2}$ tsp pepper
sprig of parsley
1 cup dry white wine
$3\frac{1}{2}$ qts water

Place the veal in a large pot with all the remaining ingredients. Cover and bring to a boil. Skim off the foam and gently simmer, covered, until the meat is tender, about 1½ hours. (Vitello Tonnato is often made by braising the meat instead of simmering it; however, the latter method is most popular in Italy.) Remove the veal from the pot, reserving the stock. Brown the veal slightly under the broiler—about 5 minutes. Cool it at room temperature, then chill in the refrigerator. Meanwhile, strain the stock and make the sauce.

Tuna Sauce

2 7-oz cans tuna, drained	¼ tsp salt
1 2-oz tin anchovy fillets in oil	¼ tsp pepper
	4 cups strained veal stock
1 cup finely chopped celery	2 cups mayonnaise
	2 Tbsp lemon juice
¼ cup finely chopped carrots	2 Tbsp drained capers
	parsley

Put the drained tuna in a saucepan with the anchovy fillets, celery, carrots, salt, pepper, and 4 cups of the stock in which the veal cooked. Simmer mixture for 20 minutes or so until the vegetables are cooked and the liquid is reduced to half. The mixture at this point should be thick. Cool. Purée the tuna-vegetable mixture in a blender. Combine the purée with the mayonnaise, lemon juice, and drained capers. Refrigerate sauce.

Cut the veal in thin slices and take the meat and tuna sauce to the picnic in separate containers. Before serving, arrange the veal slices on a large platter and spoon the sauce over them. Garnish with a few sprigs of parsley. This dish deserves a pretty presentation.

Meatloaf in Pastry Crust

The pre-game tailgate picnic must be quick and easy to serve with a minimum of fuss. It doesn't have to be dull. This on-the-wing lunch, unfolding near the stadium, can be short but savory. Try this wonderfully different pâté-style meatloaf—a sophisticated blend of veal, pork, and ham wrapped in pastry crust and sliced cold. It's complemented by a superlative Mustard Sauce.

½ lb lean salt pork
¾ lb lean veal
¾ lb lean pork
¾ lb cooked ham cut in 1-inch chunks
2 Tbsp Madeira or dry sherry
2 Tbsp cognac
¼ tsp thyme
¼ tsp tarragon
¼ tsp rosemary
¼ tsp pepper
1 Tbsp minced parsley
1½ packages piecrust mix
1 egg yolk, beaten
1 Tbsp water

Ask the butcher to grind together the salt pork (choose the kind with a strip of meat in it), veal, and lean pork. Have it ground twice. Mix the ground meat with the cubed, cooked ham, the Madeira or sherry, cognac, thyme, tarragon, rosemary, pepper, and parsley. Blend well and shape into a loaf to fit a 9- by 5- by 3-inch pan. Prepare the piecrust mix according to package directions; roll out dough on a floured board. Divide dough so you have enough for two rectangles; one 15 by 10 inches for bottom and sides of pan, and one 9 by 5 inches for top of loaf. (The package and a half of piecrust mix will give you plenty of dough to work with; roll the pastry out a little thicker than the usual ⅛ inch used for pies.) Grease the meatloaf pan, and grease a length of foil paper enough larger than the pan to extend over the rim of pan 1 inch. Put the greased side of the foil down in the pan, shaping foil to fit. Carefully line foil-lined loaf pan with the 15- by 10-inch rectangle of pastry, bringing dough up to the rim of pan. Put in the meatloaf and cover with the pastry top, pinching edges to seal. Cut several slits in top crust to let steam escape; brush top with beaten egg yolk combined with 1 Tbsp water, and bake loaf for 1½ hours at 350°. Remove from oven, cool, and chill in refrigerator. When you're ready to serve, lift loaf from pan (it's no trick with the foil paper) and cut in ½-inch slices. Serve with Mustard Sauce (see following recipe).

Despite the length of the recipe, this is not difficult to make. The only trick is measuring the pastry to fit, and this isn't a trick but an exact science if you use a ruler.

Mustard Sauce

3 Tbsp dry mustard	½ cup water
2 Tbsp sugar	1 Tbsp butter
1 Tbsp cornstarch	¼ cup white vinegar
1 tsp salt	¼ cup heavy whipping cream
1 egg yolk	

Mix the dry mustard, sugar, cornstarch, and salt. Beat the egg yolk, add the water, and stir into the dry ingredients. Cook over a low flame, stirring constantly, until mixture thickens, about 5 minutes. Remove from heat and stir in the butter and vinegar. Cool. Whip the cream until stiff and fold into mustard mixture. Keep sauce cold until ready for serving.

Eggplant Salad

A rare and subtle eggplant salad to share a plate with the Meatloaf in Pastry Crust.

3 medium-sized eggplants
1 Tbsp salt
1 Tbsp lemon juice
¼ cup minced green onions
1 cup diced celery
½ cup chopped walnuts

FRENCH DRESSING
4 Tbsp wine vinegar
6 Tbsp olive oil
1 tsp salt
½ tsp black pepper
6 Tbsp sour cream

Peel the eggplant and cut into 1-inch cubes. Simmer in boiling water containing 1 Tbsp each salt and lemon juice. When eggplant is tender, about 10 minutes, drain and cool. Mix eggplant with the green onions, celery, and walnuts; add French dressing (ingredients make ½ cup). Chill salad in refrigerator. Garnish each serving with 1 Tbsp sour cream, added at the last minute.

CHAPTER III

Grandstand Snacks

The strenuous spectator sport of vendor-hailing demands perfect timing, powerful lungs, and a ruthless will to win. Vendors are notoriously myopic and must be flagged down by a judo chop. If you win this game your trophy is one rubbery hot dog (of dubious pedigree) on a cold, stale bun.

There is, of course, a simpler way to avert starvation. Take a picnic, a grandstand snack. There are a variety of finger foods that are certainly more succulent than the commercial dog or burger.

Grandstand snacks can be grand, but they must be compact and easy to eat. There's little room in the bleachers for elbows, let alone cutlery.

Despite its restrictions, the grandstand picnic can be a petite feast. Consider the number of refreshing or warming soups that travel in a thermos, as well as the delectable snacks that unwrap as easily as a sandwich.

No need to be a victim of vendors' whims. Here are fourteen ways to beat the hot-dog game.

Gazpacho Soup

When the temperature soars at the great American ball game, a thermos of icy-cold Spanish soup will revive your spirits. It's light, zesty, and marvelously refreshing.

3 **hard-cooked eggs**
2 **Tbsp olive oil**
1 **clove garlic, crushed**
1½ **tsp Worcestershire sauce**
1 **tsp dry mustard**
2 **shakes Tabasco sauce**
juice of 1 lemon or 2 limes
salt and pepper to taste

1½ **qts tomato juice or sieved pulp of canned tomatoes**
1 **cucumber, finely minced**
1 **red onion, chopped fine**
1 **green pepper, chopped fine**
3 **strips pimento**

Sieve the yolks of the hard-cooked eggs and mix with the olive oil to make a smooth paste with the crushed garlic, Worcestershire sauce, dry mustard, Tabasco, and lemon or lime juice. Blend with the tomato juice or sieved tomato pulp. Add salt and pepper to taste, and the minced cucumber, chopped red onion, green pepper, the hard-cooked egg whites, diced, and the pimento. (All the vegetables must be cut fine enough to pass through the neck of a thermos. If possible, use a wide-necked thermos for easier pouring.) Chill the soup in the refrigerator for at least 3 hours. Gazpacho must be icy-cold. We suggest you take along some Cheese Cubes (see Index) to sprinkle on top of the soup just before serving. They add a flavorful touch.

Salmon Quiche

For a snack to accompany the Gazpacho, make a Salmon Quiche. This is a salmon pie using canned salmon that's superlative hot or cold. Cut it in convenient-sized squares or wedges.

1 package piecrust mix
2 Tbsp butter
3 Tbsp minced green onions
1-lb can pink or red salmon
2 tsp dill weed

½ tsp salt
1 Tbsp minced parsley
4 eggs
2 Tbsp dry sherry
1 cup heavy cream

Prepare piecrust mix as directed on the package and line the bottom of a 9-inch greased pie pan. Melt the butter and sauté the green onions for a few minutes. Drain the salmon (reserve the liquid, which will be about ¼ cup) and remove the skin and bones. Flake the salmon fine into a mixing bowl and add the sautéed green onions, the dill weed, salt, and parsley. Beat the eggs lightly and add to salmon mixture with the sherry and the liquid from the can. These ingredients can be stirred in by hand or mixed in a blender. Scald the cream and pour it into the salmon mixture. Pour into uncooked piecrust. Bake at 375° for about 40 minutes, or until the quiche is puffed and brown. If served cold, this will lose its souffle' quality but none of its flavor; it can be made the day before, wrapped in foil, and kept in the refrigerator.

Cream of Almond Soup

A festive party soup to team with Cold Chicken Newport (see Index), especially in crisp football weather. Nobody will ever guess it's made in a matter of minutes—about five!

2 Tbsp butter
2 Tbsp flour
3 cups chicken stock
1¼ cups ground blanched white almonds

3 cups heavy cream
1 tsp salt
½ tsp paprika
2 tsp grated lemon rind

Melt the butter and stir in the flour. Cook for 1 minute, then slowly add the chicken stock; cook, stirring, until smooth and blended, about 5 minutes. Add the almonds, heavy cream, salt, and paprika, and heat but do not let boil. Garnish with the grated lemon rind. Keep in a thermos.

Turnover Lorraine

A jewel of a non-sweet turnover, elegant enough to take to the royal enclosure at Ascot, and hearty enough to relish in the bleachers at the ballpark.

2 packages of refrigerated Crescent Dinner Rolls	1 tsp olive oil
	1 Tbsp chopped parsley
5 anchovy fillets packed in oil	1 tsp chopped chives
	2 Tbsp brandy
1 clove garlic	1 cup chopped ham
6 green onions, chopped	2 Tbsp creamed butter
4 peppercorns	1 egg yolk, beaten
1 tsp oil from anchovies	

In a mortar, mash together the anchovy fillets (reserve the oil), garlic, green onions, and peppercorns. Add 1 tsp oil from anchovies, the olive oil, parsley, chives, and brandy. Stir in the chopped ham, creamed butter, and beaten egg yolk. Let mixture stand for ½ hour. Shape the raw dough from 2 packages of Crescent Dinner Rolls into a ball, and roll out the dough on a floured board into a large square about ⅛ inch thick. Cut into 4-inch squares, put 1 heaping Tbsp of the mixture into the center of each square, and fold each over into a turnover, pressing the edges together with a fork. Bake in a medium oven (350°) for 15 minutes, or until pastry is golden brown.

Summer Tomato Soup

Here is a *fresh* tomato soup—from blender to thermos without cooking! It is a culinary sonnet to the incomparable flavor of tomatoes fresh from the vine—an icy soup blended with sour cream and a whisper of curry.

12 large, very ripe tomatoes
6 green onions, chopped
1 Tbsp salt
1 tsp sugar
½ tsp marjoram
½ tsp thyme

2 Tbsp lime juice
2 tsp grated lime peel
1½ cups sour cream
1 tsp curry powder
minced parsley

Peel the tomatoes, chop coarsely, and put in a blender, together with green onions, salt, sugar, marjoram, thyme, lime juice, and lime peel. Blend until mixture is a purée, then add sour cream and curry powder. Chill in the refrigerator. Garnish with minced parsley and pour into a thermos.

Cheese Cubes

A great nibble to enjoy with Summer Tomato Soup. These zesty Cheese Cubes are actually handsomely flavored bread cubes.

1 loaf unsliced white bread
2 eggs
4 Tbsp melted butter
¼ cup grated Parmesan
cheese

½ tsp salt
½ tsp paprika
½ tsp dry mustard

Cut the bread into slices 1 inch thick. Remove crusts and cut bread into 1-inch cubes. Beat the eggs and combine with melted butter. Mix the Parmesan cheese with the salt, paprika, and mustard. Dip the bread cubes into the egg-butter mixture. Then roll them in the cheese mixture. Place the cubes on a buttered cookie sheet and bake until golden brown, about ½ hour, turning to brown them on all sides.

Swiss Snack

Make this Swiss cheese snack wrapped in pastry with your favorite piecrust, or use the crescent dinner rolls from the refrigerated foods section of the market.

1 package piecrust mix, or	6 oz Swiss cheese, sliced
2 packages Crescent Dinner Rolls	3 Tbsp Dijon mustard
	1 egg, beaten

Prepare piecrust mix according to directions and roll out ⅛ inch thick on a floured board. Or pat 2 packages crescent-dinner-roll dough into a ball and roll out ⅛ inch thick on a floured board. Cut piecrust or dinner-roll dough into 3½-inch sqs. Place a 2½-inch triangle of Swiss cheese, dabbed with ¼ tsp Dijon mustard, on each square, and fold dough over into a triangle. Press edges together with a fork. Brush triangles with beaten egg and bake in hot oven (425 °) until pastry is golden brown, about 15 minutes.

Pizza à la Romana

Romans eat pizzas anywhere—on a Vespa, in the shower, on the street corner, or in the grandstand at a soccer game. The Neapolitans invented this famous pie, but the Romans make it better—or at least richer. Everything goes on a pizza; spread with a lavish hand. The following is one of the tastier and less elaborate varieties of Roman pizza— imagine what an elaborate one is like! Don't be discouraged by the length of the recipe—it will take less time than you think.

1 package active dry yeast
¾ cup warm water
1½ Tbsp salad oil
2 cups flour
¾ tsp salt
3 red onions, cut into rings
1 clove garlic, chopped fine
4 Tbsp olive oil
6 ripe tomatoes, peeled and
coarsely chopped
1 cup grated Parmesan
cheese

1 tsp salt
½ tsp pepper
½ tsp oregano
½ tsp basil
1 6½-oz can tuna (preferably
the Italian variety packed
in olive oil)
25 to 30 pitted black Italian
or Greek olives
2 hard-cooked eggs, chopped

Combine the yeast with the warm water and salad oil. Stir to dissolve. Add the flour and the ¾ tsp salt; knead on a floured board until dough is smooth, about 7 or 8 minutes. Put the dough in a greased bowl, cover with a cloth, and let rise until it doubles in size, about 1 hour. Cook the onion rings and garlic in the olive oil until onions are tender and transparent. In another saucepan, cook the tomatoes until they have the consistency of a lumpy sauce, about 15 minutes. Remove the dough from the bowl, put it on a floured board, and pat it down. Cover with a towel for 5 minutes. Roll out the dough into a circle about 15 inches in diameter—to fit the dimensions of a pizza pan or other pan this size. Line the pan with the pizza dough. Sprinkle the dough with the grated Parmesan cheese. Spoon the onion-garlic mixture over the dough. Season the tomato mixture with salt, pepper, oregano, and basil, and spoon this over the onion mixture. Flake and separate the tuna with a fork. Do not drain. Sprinkle the tuna and the olive oil it is packed in over the pizza. (If you use American tuna, drain and add 1 Tbsp olive oil.) Top the entire production with the pitted black olives. Bake in a 400° oven until crust is brown and pizza is bubbling, 15 or 20 minutes. Remove from oven and decorate with chopped hard-cooked eggs.

Cut the pizza into serving pieces and wrap tightly in foil— unless you want to eat it at home.

Pork Taco

This Mexican "sandwich," once considered peon food, has been adopted by the gringos. In the West, the taco is a standard item on lunch-counter menus, but the best ones are homemade. Make yours the Mexican way, starting with Carnitas, a tender, succulent pork that is the principal ingredient of this tortilla sandwich.

Carnitas

5-lb pork shoulder with bone	**½ tsp crushed coriander**
2 tsp salt	**2 onions, chopped**
½ tsp oregano	**2 carrots, chopped**
½ tsp ground cumin	

Rub the pork with the salt, oregano, cumin, and coriander. Put the pork in a large pot and barely cover with water. Add the onions and carrots. Bring the water to a boil, skim off the foam, cover the pan, and simmer for 2 hours. Remove pork and put it in a pan in the oven for another hour, until the meat is nicely browned and falling-apart tender. Cut into shredded chunks.

Corn Tortillas

These are available in most supermarkets. (You *could* learn to make your own, but tortilla-making is quite an art, requiring "Mexican palms.") Moisten 12 corn tortillas with a little water and fry in an ungreased frying pan, turning them every few seconds until they are soft enough to fold in half. Fill each tortilla with 1 Tbsp Carnitas or more, a little shredded lettuce, and a few pieces of chopped tomatoes. If you like, add 1 Tbsp green chopped onions and 1 Tbsp of shredded cheddar cheese to each. Wrap tortillas immediately in a double layer of foil and put them in an insulated bag to keep them from drying out. They'll stay warm at least 2 hours. For a hot accent, shake a little Tabasco sauce or Taco sauce inside the taco just before you eat it.

P. S. Don't forget the beer to quench the fire!

Stuffed Zucchini

Who would guess that zucchini makes a marvelous finger food to munch in the bleachers? Never has this happy squash tasted more inviting than with this seasoned meat stuffing. You need a round apple corer and a little patience, but the the results are worth the trouble.

12 small, tender zucchini	**2 Tbsp Parmesan cheese**
½ lb ground round steak	**1 egg, beaten**
½ lb ground pork loin	**½ cup stale bread, crumbled, dipped in water, and squeezed out**
1 clove garlic, minced	
2 Tbsp olive oil	
½ cup chopped parsley	**3 Tbsp olive oil**

Wash the zucchini; cut off the tips from both ends. With a round apple corer, remove the centers, leaving tubular shells open at both ends. In a bowl, combine the round steak, pork loin, garlic, olive oil, parsley, Parmesan cheese, beaten egg, and bread. Stuff the zucchini with this mixture and place them in a well-oiled, shallow pan. Brush liberally with olive oil and bake in a slow oven (325°) for about 1 hour and 15 minutes. Cold or hot, this dish is special.

Chinese Meatballs

Meatballs with an Oriental accent. The surprise ingredient, water chestnuts, teams with pork to make a mouthwatering morsel to take to the grandstand, or to a five-hour Chinese movie.

1½ **lb ground pork loin**	1 **egg, slightly beaten**
8 **water chestnuts (canned)**	1 **tsp salt**
¼ **cup minced green onions**	½ **cup breadcrumbs**
2 **Tbsp soy sauce**	

Have the butcher grind the pork loin (with all fat removed) together with the peeled and cooked water chestnuts from the can. Add the green onions, soy sauce, beaten egg, salt, and breadcrumbs. Stir well, blending ingredients, and shape into small balls, 1½ inches in diameter. Bake in a hot oven, (450°) until meatballs are cooked and lightly browned, about 20 minutes.

Portofino Sandwich

A joyous sandwich with the singing flavor and fragrance of the Mediterranean. It's accented with sunny Italian spices—garlic, basil, oregano—and olive oil. The filling: lush red tomatoes, Bel Paese cheese, anchovy fillets, black Italian olives, pimento, and onion. All this goes on a "crust-shattering" loaf of Italian or French bread. (An Italian friend of mine determines a good continental bread by whether the crust shatters when you slice it.)

1 **long loaf French or Italian bread**	1 **2-oz can anchovy fillets, drained**
1 **clove garlic, split**	8 **black Italian or Greek olives, pitted**
5 **or 6 slices Bel Paese cheese**	
3 **slices red onion, peeled and separated into rings**	1 **Tbsp olive oil**
	1 **Tbsp wine vinegar**
3 **large ripe tomatoes, sliced**	½ **tsp basil**
3 **whole pimentos, cut in half**	½ **tsp oregano**

Cut the loaf of bread in half lengthwise and rub the inside with garlic. Arrange slices of Bel Paese cheese along one half of the cut loaf. Top the cheese with the onion rings, tomato slices, pimentos, anchovy fillets, and black olives. Over this filling, sprinkle the olive oil, vinegar, basil, and oregano. Top with the other half of the loaf. Slice loaf into six equal portions and wrap in foil.

Italian Omelet

A zesty, country-style Italian omelet that you can eat in your fingers. It's equally delicious hot or cold.

3 Tbsp olive oil	1 cup finely chopped raw
½ cup thinly sliced onions	spinach (½ lb)
1 clove garlic, minced	⅓ cup grated Parmesan
2 tomatoes, peeled and	cheese
chopped	1 Tbsp chopped parsley
6 mushrooms, sliced	2 tsp salt
12 eggs, beaten	½ tsp pepper

Pour the olive oil into a 10-inch skillet and sauté the onions and garlic until golden brown. Add the tomatoes and cook until soft; stir in the mushrooms and cook another minute or so. In a bowl, combine the beaten eggs, raw spinach, Parmesan cheese, and parsley; stir well. Pour into the skillet and cook over low heat for a few minutes, loosening the omelet around the edges with a spatula, until the eggs are set. Remove from heat and run the skillet pan under the broiler for 6 minutes, or until the top is golden. Slide the omelet out onto a plate, cut in 6 wedges, and wrap in foil.

Cold Chicken Newport

This rates box seats—or at least reserved seats. Make it when you want something special for a grandstand party picnic. It's a glorious chicken fashioned of finely chopped white meat, mushrooms, delicate seasonings, and loads of butter. Shaped into patties, it's breaded and sautéed.

4 whole raw chicken breasts, boned and skinned	**6 canned mushroom caps, chopped**
½ tsp nutmeg	**2 cups seasoned flour**
2 tsp salt	**2 eggs, beaten**
ground black pepper to taste	**2 cups breadcrumbs**
½ tsp tarragon	**minced parsley**
8 Tbsp butter	**8 Tbsp butter**

Have butcher bone and skin 4 whole chicken breasts. Chop chicken fine with a knife, as for croquettes. Season with the nutmeg, salt, pepper, and tarragon. Melt 8 Tbsp butter; add the mushroom caps and chicken. Chill in refrigerator an hour (the butter acts as a binding agent). Shape mixture into 12 patties; dip each into seasoned flour, then into beaten eggs, then into breadcrumbs seasoned with a little minced parsley. Pat patties until the crumbs adhere. Melt 8 Tbsp butter and sauté the patties until golden brown on each side, about 15 minutes. Drain on paper towel. Chill and serve cold.

CHAPTER IV

Picnics Afloat

Some picnics go to sea. The picnic underway comes up from the galley hot and hearty, or cold and serene, depending on the weather. Nippy breezes stimulate sailor-sized appetites that relish a filling casserole or warming mug of soup. Sultry days call for refreshing, cold foods kept chilled in a portable cooler to lessen the load on the galley refrigerator.

Hot or cold, picnics afloat must be shipshape. As every good galley slave knows, there's no room below for confusion, elaborate preparations, or mountainous dishwashing. Everything down to the last scraped carrot must be prepared at home and taken to the boat ready to serve. This includes precooked casseroles, which are easily reheated on an asbestos pad on top of an alcohol, butane, or kerosene stove. (Use a foil-lined shallow casserole for quicker warming.) Boat ovens afford a little baking, but fuel is limited and meals must be measured in minutes.

Stick to one-plate casseroles, salads, or cold cuts that

are easy on the dishwasher—you. Steer clear of fiery foods that provoke an unquenchable thirst. Drinking water is a priceless beverage at sea, as is cold beer in quantity, since refrigeration is limited.

While the floatable picnic has restrictions, consider its dimensions! The convenience of a galley stove offers a broad latitude of picnic dishes. Here is a chapter of seaworthy recipes, many of which were given to me by members of the Balboa Yacht Club in Newport Beach, California.

Cold Clam Bisque

What could be more refreshing under sail than an icy-cold clam bisque?

3 7½-oz cans minced clams	¼ tsp thyme
1½ tsp celery salt	3½ cups heavy cream
¼ tsp cayenne	3 Tbsp chopped chives

Put the minced clams with their liquid in a blender. Add the celery salt, cayenne, thyme, and 1 cup finely chopped ice. Blend until almost smooth. Remove cover and pour in the heavy cream while blender is going. Blend for another minute. Sprinkle the soup with chopped chives before serving.

Galley Potage

Have a mug of hot potato soup flavored with ripe tomatoes! Galley Potage is a lively blend of two tasty vegetables—just the cozy soup you want when it's chilly on deck.

3 cups thinly sliced potatoes	2 tsp sugar
2 onions, peeled and sliced thin	1½ tsp salt
	½ tsp paprika
6 Tbsp butter	½ tsp chervil
6 cups sliced, peeled fresh tomatoes, or 3½ cups canned tomatoes	½ tsp basil
	6 cups beef bouillon
	2 cups heavy cream

Peel and slice enough potatoes to make 3 cups. Put them in cold water to prevent discoloration. Meanwhile, sauté the onions in the butter until tender—10 or 15 minutes. Add the tomatoes and simmer 20 minutes, covered. Drain the potatoes and add, along with the bouillon. Cook until potatoes are soft and very tender. Let soup cool to tepid, then put in blender for a few minutes until it is puréed. Add the heavy cream. Reheat and put in a thermos.

Cold Shrimp in Pastry Shell

These are the best cold shrimp you'll ever serve. They're dressed in an enticing, green-flecked mayonnaise sauce and served in puff-paste shells. This out-of-the-ordinary party dish is a good deal easier to make than it looks. What more could a hostess in dungarees ask?

3 lb medium-sized fresh shrimp	6 puff-paste pastry shells (these are available frozen)

Boil the shrimp in water to cover for 5 minutes; cool, shell, and devein shrimp. Bake the pastry shells according to package directions.

Mayonnaise Sauce

¼ cup chopped parsley	1 egg yolk
¼ cup chopped watercress	1 Tbsp tarragon vinegar
¼ cup shredded fresh spinach	1 Tbsp lemon juice
2 green onions, sliced	½ tsp salt
1 clove garlic, sliced	¼ tsp pepper
2 tsp dry mustard	¾ cup mayonnaise
	½ cup sour cream

In a blender, combine the parsley, watercress, and spinach; blend for 1 minute. Turn off motor, push greens down into the blades, and add green onions, garlic, dry mustard, egg yolk, tarragon vinegar, lemon juice, salt, and pepper; blend for another 30 seconds or so. Add the mayonnaise and sour cream and blend again for 30 seconds. Chill. When you are ready to serve, stir the cold shrimp into sauce and spoon into the pastry shells (preferably warm).

Clam Chowder Pie

A unique variation of traditional chowder. It combines the usual ingredients but is a little richer and a little clammier. If you can make this with fresh clams, please do.

3 **large potatoes**
3 **medium-sized onions, sliced**
2 **8-oz bottles clam juice (or more)**
6 **Tbsp butter**
6 **Tbsp flour**
2 **cups light cream**
3 **8-oz cans chopped clams, drained, or 36 fresh clams**

3 **7-oz cans whole Little Neck clams, drained, or 24 fresh clams**
salt to taste
1½ **cups Saltine cracker crumbs**
2 **Tbsp butter**

Peel the potatoes and cut them into ¼-inch slices. Simmer the potatoes and onions in the clam juice for 10 minutes, or until tender. Drain, reserving the broth. (If there is less than 1 cup, you'll need more clam juice to make up the cup. The liquid varies with the length of time you cook the potatoes and their size). In a large saucepan, melt 6 Tbsp butter and stir in the flour. Cook for 1 minute, then gradually stir in the cream to make a thick cream sauce. Add 1 cup of reserved broth. Stir the sauce and add the chopped clams and whole Little Neck clams and the cooked potatoes and onions. Salt to taste. Simmer 2 or 3 minutes. Transfer to a buttered casserole and sprinkle the top with

Saltine crumbs. Dot with 2 Tbsp butter and bake in 350 °
oven until crumbs are lightly browned.

Balboa Ham Loaf

Come squall or calm, this cold ham loaf is ready any
time you are. Simply slice and serve. No wonder it ships
out on so many sloops! It is a special favorite with ocean-
racing sailors.

2 lb lean cooked ham, ground
3 Tbsp minced green onions
½ cup shredded Swiss cheese
1 egg, beaten
2 tsp prepared mustard
1 3-oz can sliced mushrooms,
   drained

¼ cup sour cream
1 ½ packages of piecrust
   mix
1 egg, beaten with 1 Tbsp
   water

In a mixing bowl, combine the ham, green onions, Swiss
cheese, beaten egg, prepared mustard, sliced mushrooms,
and sour cream. Blend well; chill for 15 minutes while you
make the piecrust. Prepare piecrust mix according to package directions, roll out dough on a floured board, cut into
two 6- by 14-inch rectangles. Put one rectangle on an ungreased baking sheet. Shape the ham mixture into a loaf
about 3 inches in diameter and place the loaf in the center of the rectangle on the baking sheet. Fold pastry up
around the sides of the loaf (it will reach only halfway.)
Brush the outside edges of the dough lightly with egg beaten
with water. Fit the second rectangle over the top of the
loaf, pressing against the bottom section of pastry to seal.
Prick loaf with a fork in several places to let steam escape.
Brush pastry with beaten egg. Bake in a 350° oven for 40
minutes, or until crust is golden. Serve with additional
sour cream if you desire.

Mozzarella in Carrozza

Literally translated, the name means "mozzarella cheese in a carriage," the carriage being a casing of sandwich bread. Call it a sandwich or call it a meal, it's certainly a picnic Neapolitan style. Prepare it at home and take it to the boat ready to fry and serve in a few minutes. There is a sauce to top it, but it's not imperative.

12 slices white bread with crust removed	$\frac{1}{2}$ cup milk
	$\frac{1}{2}$ cup dry breadcrumbs
6 slices fresh mozzarella cheese, $\frac{1}{8}$ inch thick	2 eggs
	2 Tbsp heavy cream
6 slices Bel Paese cheese, $\frac{1}{8}$ inch thick	1 pt cooking oil
6 slices Fontina or Taleggio cheese, $\frac{1}{8}$ inch thick	

Cut the bread into $3\frac{1}{2}$-inch rounds and the cheese slices into $3\frac{1}{4}$-inch rounds. Make 6 sandwiches, combining the three cheeses in each. Dip sandwiches into milk briefly and press the edges of the bread together to seal. Next dip into breadcrumbs so the sandwiches are thoroughly coated. At this point wrap the sandwiches in foil to take to the boat. When you're ready to fry them, beat the eggs with the heavy cream, dip the sandwiches in the egg mixture, and deep-fry them in cooking oil heated to 375° until golden brown on each side. Drain on paper towels and serve hot. If you want the sauce, it can be made at home and briefly reheated.

Sauce

$\frac{1}{4}$ lb unsalted butter	2 tsp capers, chopped
4 flat anchovies, chopped fine	1 Tbsp finely chopped parsley
2 tsp lemon juice	

Melt the butter and stir in the anchovies, lemon juice, capers, and parsley. Heat and pour over the sandwiches.

Ratatouille

A glamorous dish to dress up an otherwise pedestrian picnic. Simply translated, Ratatouille is an eggplant-tomato-zucchini casserole that can be served cold. It's easier to make than to pronounce.

2 **medium-sized unpeeled eggplants, cubed**	2 **onions, sliced thin**
2 **large unpeeled zucchini, sliced thin**	1 **clove garlic, crushed**
	6 **tomatoes, peeled**
1 ½ **tsp salt**	½ **tsp salt**
4 **Tbsp olive oil**	½ **tsp pepper**
2 **green peppers, seeded and sliced**	2 **Tbsp chopped parsley**
	sour cream (optional)

Sprinkle the cubed eggplant and sliced zucchini with 1½ tsp salt and let stand for 1 hour. Rinse and dry on paper towels. Sauté these vegetables a few pieces at a time, in the olive oil (use a little oil at a time), until lightly brown. In another pan, sauté the green peppers, onions, and garlic. Add a little more olive oil if you need it. Cut the tomatoes into quarters, chop fine, and add to the green peppers and onions. Season with ½ tsp salt and pepper, and sauté until tomatoes are tender, a few minutes. Place a layer of this mixture in the bottom of a casserole and sprinkle with 1 Tbsp chopped parsley. Spoon a layer of eggplant and zucchini over tomatoes and repeat, ending with tomato layer on top. Sprinkle with remaining Tbsp chopped parsley. Bake in a moderate oven (350°) for 35 minutes. Serve cold. We like this with a dab of sour cream topping, but that's optional.

Potato Pie Provençal

A gourmet touch for a routine steak-and-salad menu. Hot or cold, this is a potato of distinction.

1 package piecrust mix
1 lb cottage cheese (small curd)
2 cups mashed potatoes (instant mashed potatoes can be used)
½ cup sour cream
2 eggs, lightly beaten
2 tsp salt
¼ tsp pepper
2 Tbsp chives
½ cup thinly sliced green onions
4 Tbsp grated cheddar cheese
1 Tbsp paprika

Prepare piecrust mix according to package directions and line a 9-inch greased pie plate with the dough. In a mixing bowl, stir together the cottage cheese, mashed potatoes, sour cream, beaten eggs, salt, pepper, chives, and green onions. Pour mixture into pastry-lined pie plate and sprinkle top with cheddar cheese and paprika. Bake in a hot oven (450°) until piecrust is cooked, about 40 to 50 minutes.

White Veal Stew

The always welcome stew is a picnic for the galley slave. It can be heated in a matter of minutes. This delicately seasoned ragout of veal is party fare.

3 lb boneless veal shoulder, cut in 1-inch chunks
1 onion stuck with 2 cloves
2 tsp salt
2 sprigs parsley
1 bay leaf
½ tsp thyme
1 carrot, chopped
16 whole small white onions, peeled
1 lb small fresh mushroom caps
½ tsp lemon juice
5 Tbsp butter
5 Tbsp flour
2 egg yolks, lightly beaten
2 tsp lemon juice
¾ cup heavy cream

In a large pot containing 1½ qts water, put the veal, the onion stuck with cloves, the salt, parsley, bay leaf, thyme, and carrot. Bring to a boil, skim off foam, cover pot, and simmer for 1 hour. Add the small white onions and continue cooking for another ½ hour, or until meat is tender. Remove veal and small onions from stock. Strain 3 cups of stock, return to the large pot, and add the ½ tsp lemon juice. Simmer the mushroom caps in the stock for 2 or 3 minutes. In a saucepan, melt the butter, blend the flour, stir in the stock and cook until gravy is consistency of cream sauce; add the mushrooms, onions, and veal; heat gently. Now comes the final masterful touch that gives this dish its exquisite flavor. Beat 2 egg yolks lightly with the 2 tsp lemon juice and the heavy cream. Stir into this a little warm gravy, add mixture to the stew, and stir. When you reheat this on the galley stove, do not let it boil — just warm it gently.

Hungarian Goulash

The Hungarians don't have an ocean, but they have a great ocean-going stew. Goulash is rich, savory, and a picnic in a pot. There's more to goulash than paprika.

3 lb boneless pork tenderloin	1 green pepper, chopped
4 Tbsp flour	2 tomatoes, peeled and chopped
2 tsp salt	1½ cups water (or more)
2 tsp Hungarian paprika	6 small new potatoes, peeled
¼ tsp cayenne pepper	1 1-lb can sauerkraut
4 Tbsp butter	1 pt sour cream
1 onion, chopped fine	1 Tbsp caraway seeds
1 clove garlic, minced	

Cut pork into 1-inch cubes. Combine the flour, salt, Hungarian paprika, and cayenne pepper in a bowl. Dredge and roll the meat in the flour mixture and brown it in a skillet in the butter. Add the onion, garlic, green pepper, tomatoes, and 1½ cups of water. Cover skillet and simmer 15 minutes. Add more water if necesary. Put in the potatoes and continue simmering for another 30 minutes, or until pork is fork tender. Drain the sauerkraut and rinse well with cold water; combine with the goulash, and pour into a casserole. Stir in the sour cream and sprinkle with caraway seeds. Bake in a medium oven (350°) for ½ hour.

Green Pepper Pot

Not least among the virtues of this lively green pepper and ground meat casserole is its cost. It will feed a hungry crew of 6 for under $3.00, and there is nothing pinch-penny about the taste.

3 Tbsp butter
1½ cups raw, long-grained white rice
3 chicken bouillon cubes
3 cups boiling water
3 green peppers, seeded and cut in ½-inch slices
2 Tbsp butter
1½ lb ground round steak
one onion, chopped

2 ribs celery, sliced thin
1 clove garlic, minced
1 tsp oregano
1 tsp basil
1 tsp salt
½ tsp pepper
2 8-oz cans tomato sauce
1 cup shredded cheddar cheese

Melt 3 Tbsp butter in a skillet and add the rice; stir until rice is lightly browned. Transfer rice to a large, shallow, greased casserole. Dissolve the bouillon cubes in the boiling water and pour over the rice. Lay the green pepper slices on top of the rice. Cover casserole, put it in the oven, and bake 20 minutes at 375°. Meanwhile, melt 2 Tbsp butter and brown the meat for 5 minutes; add the onion, celery, garlic, oregano, basil, salt, and pepper. Stir in the tomato sauce. Remove casserole from oven and spoon the meat-tomato mixture over the green peppers and rice. Cover and continue baking for 15 minutes. Remove cover, sprinkle with shredded cheddar cheese, and bake 5 minutes uncovered.

Tortilla Chicken Casserole

A prize recipe from a Sunday sailor who vows this is one of the best casseroles afloat. It's also one of the best ashore.

1 can cream of chicken soup	12 corn tortillas, torn into
1 can cream of celery soup	small pieces
1 can chicken broth	3 cups cooked chicken, cut
1 4-oz can green chilis,	into bite-size pieces
chopped	8-oz cheddar cheese, grated

Mix together the cream of chicken soup, cream of celery soup, and chicken broth. Add the chopped chilis and tortillas. Let the tortillas soak in the mixture ½ hour. Spoon a layer of the soup-tortilla-chili mixture into a large, shallow casserole. Cover with the cooked chicken, then another layer of the mixture, and top with the grated cheddar. Bake for 25 minutes in 350° oven until casserole is hot and bubbling.

Help! Four-Extra-Guests-For-Dinner Casserole

When friends of friends just happen to turn up for a sail, don't panic. You have in the galley a casserole that e-x-p-a-n-d-s! This is a marvelous concoction of ground meat and any canned vegetables handy on the shelf, topped off with a corn-muffin crust. If you don't have an oven on board, forget the crust. The following proportions are for 6; you can expand as necessary.

2 lb ground round steak
1 onion, chopped
2 Tbsp butter
1 tsp salt
1 1-lb-12-oz can tomatoes
½ tsp basil
½ tsp thyme
1 tsp salt
½ tsp pepper
2 12-oz cans Mexicorn (corn
mixed with red and green
peppers)
1 4-oz can sliced mushrooms
1 4-oz can pitted black olives

CRUST

1 15-oz package corn-muffin
mix
1 egg, beaten
1 cup milk

Crumble the meat into a large saucepan. Add the onion, butter, and 1 tsp salt and sauté until meat is brown. Add the tomatoes, basil, thyme, 1 more tsp salt (less if you prefer), and the pepper; simmer 5 minutes. Add the Mexicorn, sliced mushrooms, and black olives; simmer another 10 to 15 minutes. Serve as is, or add a corn-muffin crust. (Follow package directions for corn muffins, stirring contents of package with the beaten egg and milk. Pour the stew into a shallow casserole, pour the batter on top, and bake in 425° oven for 25 minutes, or until crust is golden brown.

Chicken and Wild-Rice Casserole

If you have a yacht you can afford wild rice; if not, wild-rice mix will do. Yacht or rowboat, this is a beautiful casserole to take along.

½ cup butter
1 lb mushrooms, sliced
2 Tbsp chopped green
onions
2 Tbsp chopped green
pepper
¼ cup chopped blanched
almonds
3 cups cooked chicken
3 cups cooked wild rice or
wild-rice mix
3 cups chicken broth
¼ cup sauterne

Melt the butter in a large skillet and sauté the sliced mushrooms along with the green onions, green pepper, and almonds. Add the chicken, wild rice or wild-rice mix, and chicken broth, and pour the mixture into a casserole. Bake 20 minutes in a 350° oven, add the sauterne and bake another 10 minutes.

Encore Casserole

Team this hearty casserole with a mixed green salad for a meal to delight a famished crew. It never fails to win an encore, for seconds and even thirds, especially from men.

1 Tbsp butter	¾ cup sour cream
1 lb ground round steak	⅓ cup minced green onions
2 8-oz cans tomato sauce	2 Tbsp minced green pepper
1 tsp salt	8 oz package medium-sized
½ tsp pepper	noodles
½ tsp basil	2½ qts boiling water
1 cup cottage cheese	2 Tbsp salt
8 oz cream cheese, softened	2 Tbsp melted butter

Melt butter in skillet and brown the meat, crumbling it with a fork. Add the tomato sauce, 1 tsp salt, pepper, and basil. In a bowl, cream together the cottage cheese, cream cheese, sour cream, onions, and green pepper. Cook the noodles in the boiling water with 2 Tbsp salt for 8 minutes. Drain the noodles and toss with the melted butter. Place half the noodles in the bottom of a large, shallow buttered casserole. Cover with the cheese mixture. Top with the remaining noodles. Pour the meat sauce over the noodles. Bake 40 minutes at 375°.

Pea Salad

Peas on a picnic? Yes indeed, when they're prepared this unique way! These petite peas are enhanced by sour cream with an accent of crisp bacon and green onions. This is a provocative vegetable salad to serve with Captain's Ham (see Index). The peas are *not* cooked, which gives them a fresh charm.

2 packages frozen tiny peas
1 cup sour cream
6 slices crisply fried bacon, crumbled
6 green onions, sliced
½ tsp salt

Thaw the peas at room temperature, drain, combine with sour cream, crumbled bacon, green onions, and salt.

Salade Nicoise

An inspired salad for a fantail picnic is this colorful import from the French Riviera. Serve it with an icy soup on sultry days. It may be made well in advance and chilled; it keeps for hours. Serve with hot buttered French bread.

2 cups canned French-cut green beans, drained
6 small potatoes, cooked and peeled
1 green pepper, seeded and sliced
12 cherry tomatoes
1 large red onion, sliced into thin rings
3 7-oz cans tuna, drained
1 2-oz tin flat anchovies, drained
12 black pitted olives, Greek or Italian

¼ cup finely chopped parsley
3 hard-cooked eggs, quartered

DRESSING

½ cup olive oil
3 Tbsp wine vinegar
½ tsp salt
2 tsp Dijon mustard
1 clove garlic, minced
freshly ground pepper
½ tsp basil
½ tsp oregano

In a large salad bowl, combine the green beans, potatoes, green pepper, cherry tomatoes, onion rings, and tuna. Combine the ingredients for the dressing and toss the salad. Top the salad with flat anchovies, pitted black olives, parsley, and quartered hard-cooked eggs.

Mixed Fruit Ambrosia

A mixed-fruit blessing for dessert! It means an extra course and extra dishes, but it's worth it. Never has canned fruit tasted so interesting. The secret is brandy and sour cream.

1 1-lb can Royal Anne cherries

1 1-lb-13-oz can whole apricots, peeled and pitted

1 1-lb-13-oz can freestone peach halves

1 lemon, grated rind and juice

1 orange, grated rind and juice

1 cup dark brown sugar

4 Tbsp brandy

1 cup sour cream

Drain the cherries, apricots, and peach halves. Cut the apricots and peach halves in two. Mix with the cherries and put the fruit in the bottom of a shallow baking dish. Add the juice and grated rind of 1 lemon and 1 orange. Gently stir in the dark brown sugar. Bake for 10 or 15 minutes, until sugar melts. Sprinkle with the brandy. Serve cold or hot, with sour cream on the side to use as a topping.

Dockside Parties

Boat picnics also unfold dockside, when the sun is over the yardarm and the cocktail flag is hoisted. Although galley facilities are still limited, dining at anchorage is easier and widens the picnic menu to include knife-and-fork dishes.

Cold Sirloin Del Mar

This saucy, cold sirloin arrives on a large platter adorned with artichoke hearts, mushrooms, and cherry tomatoes.

3 Tbsp olive oil
juice 1 lemon
2 tsp powdered chicken stock base
1 lb fresh mushrooms, sliced
2½ lb thick sirloin steak, broiled and chilled
½ cup dry red wine
3 Tbsp red wine vinegar
4 Tbsp olive oil

¼ tsp chervil
¼ tsp thyme
¼ tsp basil
¼ tsp marjoram
½ tsp salt
¼ tsp pepper
24 cherry tomatoes
6 canned artichoke hearts, sliced

Combine the 3 Tbsp olive oil, lemon juice, and powdered chicken stock base, and sauté the mushrooms in this for about 1 minute, until mushrooms are barely tender. Drain, and reserve liquid. Slice the sirloin steak into ½-inch strips. Combine the wine, wine vinegar, 4 Tbsp olive oil, chervil, thyme, basil, marjoram, salt, and pepper. Add liquid drained from mushrooms. Marinate the steak and the mushrooms in the dressing for 2 or 3 hours. When you're ready to serve, remove the steak strips from the marinade and arrange carefully on a large platter. Spoon the mushrooms and dressing over the strips. (Reserve a little of the dressing.) Arrange the cherry tomatoes and artichoke hearts around the edge of the platter, and spoon the reserved dressing over them.

Captain's Ham

One of the prettiest hams that ever emerged from a galley, this is also one of the easiest to prepare. The glamour and flavor is in the cold glaze.

10 oz creamed cheddar
    cheese (from jar)
2 tsp prepared horseradish
3 Tbsp heavy cream
2 Tbsp chopped chives or
    green onions
½ tsp seasoned salt

2 Tbsp chopped pimento
⅓ cup chopped pitted black
    olives
3-lb pre-cooked, canned ham
parsley and pimento strips
    to garnish

Combine the cheese with the prepared horseradish and heavy cream, and mix until it is a smooth paste. Sprinkle in the chives or green onions, seasoned salt, and pimento. Stir in the chopped black olives. Spread the mixture over the top and sides of the ham. Decorate with sprigs of parsley and pimento strips. Chill until ready to serve.

Cold Roast Pork Regina

Here's a cold roast pork that's welcome aboard any time, especially for the party picnic dockside. It's sliced very thin and spread with a lovely walnut-chutney-apple mixture. Slice it for finger food or cutlery dining, as you prefer.

3-lb boneless pork tenderloin
    rolled
1 clove garlic, crushed
1 Tbsp rosemary
1 Tbsp salt
½ tsp pepper
½ cup soy sauce

2 cooking apples
2 cups water
4 pickled walnuts, chopped
    fine
2 Tbsp chutney
2 tsp lemon juice
salt and pepper to taste

Have the butcher prepare a boneless rolled pork tenderloin roast for easy slicing. Spread over it the crushed garlic, rosemary, 1 Tbsp salt, and ½ tsp pepper. Wrap the meat in foil and roast in the oven at 350° for 2 hours, basting frequently with soy sauce. Open the foil and roast another half hour. The pork should be fork-tender in 2½ hours. Cool the roast and prepare the sauce. Peel, core, and chop the cooking apples and simmer in 2 cups of water until tender. Drain, then rub apples through a strainer. Mix apple purée with the pickled walnuts, chutney, and lemon juice. Add salt and pepper to taste. Slice cold pork very thin. Spread the apple-chutney-walnut mixture on half the slices and cover each with another slice.

CHAPTER V

Pocket Picnics

Pocket picnics slip into a knapsack, glove compartment, or bicycle basket for a summer outing. The so succulent morsels, no bigger than hors d'oeuvre, quell the appetite en route, or, when multiplied, unwrap as a feast to team with a split of wine or can of beer.

These appeasing snacks have many virtues, but none greater than their ability to silence small-fry rebellion on long car trips. They're the greatest answer to that persistent, nerve-grating whine from the back seat, "When are we gonna get there?" Pocket picnics are parent savers; carry enough of these pacifying goodies to get you to your destination sweet-tempered and unshaken.

Don't be wary of snacks that are grown-up and interesting. On the road, children are more responsive to new foods and flavors. Here's your chance to let Junior discover there's more than one way to relish hamburger. Wrap it in a grape leaf and you have a dolma, a Greek delicacy that tastes familiar enough for youngsters to love yet is gourmet feasting.

Dolmas (Stuffed Grape Leaves)

1 large jar grape leaves	1 tsp salt
2 onions, chopped	½ tsp pepper
½ cup olive oil	dash cinnamon
¾ cup uncooked rice	2 Tbsp raisins
1½ lb ground round steak	½ cup white wine
1 tsp chopped mint	

Remove grape leaves from jar and rinse briefly in cold water (they're packed in brine). In a skillet, sauté the onions in the olive oil, add the rice, and stir until rice is golden. Add the meat and brown lightly. Remove from heat and combine with the mint, salt, pepper, cinnamon, and raisins. In the center of each grape leaf, put 1 Tbsp of the filling. Roll up the leaves (not too tightly) into packets, tucking in the ends. Pack the dolmas close together in a casserole and weight them down with an oven-proof plate 1 or 2 inches smaller than the casserole. Pour in the white wine and add sufficient water just to cover the plate. Cover the casserole and bake in a slow oven (300°) 40 to 45 minutes. Check and add more water if needed. When cooked, remove dolmas from casserole, wrap in foil, and carry, tightly packed, in a plastic container.

Antipasto Roll

All the delights of the antipasto rolled into one! Try your own variations on the theme, using other salamis and fillings from the antipasto tray.

12 slices Mortadella salami	2 hard-cooked eggs, chopped fine
1 6½-oz can white tuna, drained	12 ½-inch chunks Bel Paese cheese
3 Tbsp mayonnaise	

Remove the outside casing from the salami (if Mortadella isn't available in your supermarket, you can buy it in any Italian delicatessen.) Drain the tuna, moisten it with the mayonnaise, and add the chopped eggs. Spread 1 Tbsp of the mixture over each slice of salami and top with a chunk of cheese. Roll up the salami and fasten with a toothpick. Serve this pocket picnic with Giardiniera, the Italian pickled vegetables available in jars at Italian groceries.

Scotch Eggs

One of the memorable delights of English pubs, these tasty eggs wrapped in sausage are a great thirst-raiser, so don't forget to tuck a can of ale or beer in your knapsack.

6 hard-cooked eggs, peeled	¾ cup breadcrumbs
¾ lb pork sausage	3 Tbsp butter
2 eggs, beaten	

Wrap each hard-cooked egg in raw sausage meat, about ¼ inch thick. (Use the best quality sausage, preferably flavored with sage and thyme.) Dip the sausage-wrapped eggs into the beaten eggs, then dip in the breadcrumbs. Fry the eggs slowly in butter, turning continuously until sausage is cooked on all sides, about 10 minutes.

Pink Eggs

The pink pickled egg that Grandpa washed down with a nickel beer in the good old saloon days. The free lunch and nickel stein are only a sweet memory, but pink eggs are still around and good as ever!

6 hard-cooked eggs	½ bay leaf
1 cup juice from canned beets	¼ tsp ground allspice
1 cup cider vinegar	1 tsp salt
1 clove garlic, crushed	½ tsp pepper

Hard-cook the eggs according to directions for Stuffed Eggs (see Index). Put the eggs under cold water, then peel them. In a quart jar, combine all the remaining ingredients. Put in the eggs and let stand overnight. Like Scotch Eggs, these are a famous thirst-rouser. Bring the beer.

Round Celery

When you press two ribs of stuffed celery together you have round celery, a doubly delicious delicacy. The flavors blend as you happily and noisily chew this crisp pocket picnic.

24 ribs tender young celery	**2 tsp anchovy paste**
3 oz cream cheese	**3 oz blue cheese**
3 Tbsp butter	**3 Tbsp butter**

Wash and dry celery. Cut ribs into 4-inch lengths to get 24 pieces of matching size. In a bowl, cream the cream cheese with 3 Tbsp butter and the anchovy paste. In another bowl, cream the blue cheese with the other 3 Tbsp of butter. Stuff 12 pieces of celery with the cream-cheese-anchovy mixture and 12 with the blue-cheese mixture. Press together to form 12 rounds with half of each containing cream cheese, the other half blue cheese. Wrap in wax paper and chill in refrigerator.

Miniature Meatballs

The inventor of the meatball deserves a bust in the culinary hall of fame. The meatball is an immortal morsel. It teams with spaghetti, floats invitingly in soups, slices up into a robust sandwich filling, and, when impaled on a toothpick, stars as an hors d'oeuvre. It also makes a delicious pocket picnic. These miniature meatballs are as good cold as when sizzling from the chafing dish.

½ cup breadcrumbs
¼ cup milk
1 onion, chopped fine
2 Tbsp butter
2 lbs ground round steak
½ cup minced parsley
2 mint leaves, chopped fine

2 egg yolks
2 cloves garlic, minced
2 tsp salt
¼ tsp pepper
2 Tbsp olive oil
2 Tbsp butter

Soak the breadcrumbs in the milk and stir until blended. Sauté the onion in 2 Tbsp butter until transparent. In a bowl, combine the meat, breadcrumbs, onion, parsley, mint leaves, egg yolks, garlic, salt, and pepper. Shape into bite-sized meatballs and brown in a skillet in the olive oil and 2 Tbsp butter. Cook slowly until done inside, about 5 minutes. Makes about 24 meatballs.

Piroshki

Piroshki are small Russian turnovers, classically served with borscht. They're usually made with either meat or cabbage. This is a simplified version that is close enough to pass for piroshki (unless you're a White Russian).

1 medium-sized onion, chopped fine
3 Tbsp butter
1 lb ground round steak
1 tsp salt
¼ tsp pepper

2 hard-cooked eggs, chopped
½ cup cooked rice
½ cup sour cream
2 packages refrigerated Crescent Dinner Rolls

Sauté the onion in the butter, add the meat, and brown. Season with salt and pepper. Remove from heat and add the hard-cooked eggs, rice, and sour cream. Stir well. Prepare the dough from refrigerated Crescent Dinner Rolls as directed for Turnovers Lorraine (see Index). In the center of each square put 1 heaping Tbsp of meat-rice mixture and fold over into a turnover, pressing edges together with a fork. Bake in a medium oven (375°) for 15 minutes, or until pastry is golden brown.

Beef Rolls

You won't have to stop for lunch if you have these rolls in the glove compartment. They are sufficiently hearty to sooth demon appetites and tempers front seat and back. Notice the rich filling.

2 cups biscuit mix	3 green onions, chopped
1 tsp paprika	¼ cup chopped parsley
1 cup sour cream	1 Tbsp horseradish mustard
1 lb ground round steak	1 tsp salt
1 egg, beaten	¼ tsp pepper

Stir the biscuit mix with the paprika and sour cream until you can work with the dough and knead it. Separate dough into 3 equal parts, roll it out on a floured board about ⅛ inch thick. Divide each part into 3 rectangles about 5 by 4 inches each. Combine the meat with the beaten egg, green onions, parsley, horseradish mustard, salt, and pepper. Spoon meat mixture evenly over the biscuit rectangles and roll up the dough, jelly-roll fashion. With a wet knife, cut the rolls into 1-inch slices. Bake on an ungreased cookie sheet in 400° oven until brown, about ½ hour.

Stuffed Cherry Tomatoes

Cherry tomatoes are luscious right from the vine, but even tastier when stuffed with this mixture. Carry them right side up and securely wrapped.

24 small cherry tomatoes	1 tsp Worcestershire sauce
1 3-oz package chipped beef	1 Tbsp chopped chives
8 oz cream cheese, softened	chopped parsley

Core the cherry tomatoes, removing pulp and seeds. Turn them upside down to drain and chill them in the refrigerator. Chop the chipped beef fine and blend with the softened cream cheese. Season with the Worcestershire sauce and chopped chives. Stuff the mixture into the tomatoes and cover with chopped parsley. Refrigerate until you are ready to leave and double-wrap the tomatoes in foil to retain the chill.

Salt Sticks

These disappear like peanuts. They are "munchies"— smaller than a snack and bigger than your will power. You will gobble them by the dozen, so make enough.

⅔ **cup butter**
⅔ **cup vegetable shortening**
2 cups unsifted flour
2 egg yolks
1 tsp salt
2 Tbsp water

2 eggs
4 tsp milk
coarse salt (kosher variety is best)
caraway seeds

Cut the butter and vegetable shortening into the flour; add the egg yolks and 1 tsp salt. With a fork, mix in about 2 Tbsp water. Chill the dough. Roll out the dough and cut it into pencil-thick sticks about 3 inches long. Beat the eggs lightly with the milk and brush the Salt Sticks. Place on a cookie sheet, sprinkle with coarse salt and caraway seeds, and bake in 425° oven until brown, 10 to 12 minutes. This makes about 5 dozen sticks.

Walnut Sticks

You will get a lot of mileage out of these rich and satisfying "sticks," which are actually finger-width slices of bread covered with curry-flavored cream cheese and dusted with chopped walnuts.

12 slices white bread
8-oz cream cheese, softened
1 Tbsp cream
½ tsp curry powder

½ tsp lemon juice
1 cup finely chopped wal-
nuts

Cut the crusts from the bread slices and cut each slice into finger-width pieces (about 1 inch wide). Blend the softened cream cheese with the cream, curry powder, and lemon juice. Spread the cheese mixture on both sides of the bread "sticks" and dip the sticks in the finely chopped walnuts. Chill in refrigerator until ready to pack. Put a layer of wax paper between layers of Walnut Sticks and wrap securely in foil.

Friar Tuck's Toast

A savory from English taverns for the modern wayfarer—a tasty tribute to the jolly Friar.

12 slices thin white
 sandwich bread
¾ cup grated sharp cheddar
 cheese

¼ cup butter
1 tsp dry mustard
2 tsp Worcestershire sauce
6 slices bacon

Trim the crusts from the slices of bread. In a bowl, combine the cheese, butter, dry mustard, Worcestershire sauce. Cook the bacon until crisp, drain, and crumble into the cheese mixture. Spread mixture on the bread and roll up each slice like a jelly-roll, securing the rolls with toothpicks. Place under broiler to toast, turning to brown on both sides.

German Onion Cake

Among the culinary delights of the world is German Onion Cake, actually a bread filled with a sour-cream custard, which is served in October when the wine grapes are harvested. It's an inspired pocket picnic to slip into your knapsack with a split of wine and some fruit and cheese. Incidentally, German Onion Cake embellishes any picnic, as a bread or substitute for potatoes.

1 4-oz package hot-roll mix	2 cups sour cream
4 large yellow onions, peeled and sliced thin	3 eggs
	½ tsp salt
6 Tbsp butter	1 Tbsp poppy seed

Prepare the hot-roll mix according to the package directions. While the dough is rising, sauté the onion slices in the butter until onions are transparent and tender. Cool onions. Beat the sour cream with the eggs and salt and combine with the onions. When the dough has doubled in size, knead 10 seconds and let set for 10 minutes. Roll out the dough on a floured board into a 11- by 15-inch rectangle. Line a greased 9- by 13-inch pan with the dough, turning up a 1-inch edge on all sides. Pour the onion and sour-cream mixture over the dough, sprinkle with the poppy seeds, and bake in 350° oven for about 1 hour, or until golden brown on top. Cut into 3-inch squares and wrap twice in foil. Wrap again in brown wrapping paper or put in a bag to keep it moist and warm as long as possible.

CHAPTER VI

Camper Cookery

Today, "the house by the side of the road" is a house on wheels. Millions of Americans seek the adventure of mountains and sea in campers. Some campers have small kitchens; others depend on a portable camp stove and oven.

Camper cookery is inventive. It often starts with a can opener. Canned meats and vegetables, soups for sauces, instant mixes, and other "convenience foods" are essential for the improvised meal. With a little imaginative blending, a dash of wine, a pinch of herbs, you can work culinary miracles even on a camper stove.

Living off the bounty of the land is, of course, preferable to shelf dinners. Whenever possible, enjoy the local meats, fish, game, and farm-fresh vegetables in an outdoor barbecue. Who knows, you might be in venison or blue-trout country or along the coast where the clamming is great! An Americana specialty of small towns is the homemade cakes and pies available at church bazaars and school fairs.

The indoor and outdoor camper picnics listed in this section include both shelf dinners and barbecues.

Biscuit Eggs

Camper cookery is always inventive—even for breakfast. Here's an imaginative way of cooking eggs that starts with a muffin tin and a package of refrigerator biscuits.

1 package refrigerated
   biscuits
	salt and pepper to taste
	6 Tbsp grated cheddar
	   cheese

1 Tbsp butter	
6 eggs	

Separate 6 biscuits from the package. Butter a muffin tin with 1 Tbsp butter and place 1 biscuit in each of the cups, pressing down so you have a small indentation, or "well." Drop 1 raw egg into each well and sprinkle it with salt and pepper to taste and 1 Tbsp grated cheddar cheese. Bake in a moderate oven 15 or 20 minutes, or until the eggs are cooked but not hard. Loosen the biscuits around the edges and remove gently.

Barbecued Lime Chicken

The queen of the picnic table is still chicken, but all too frequently it is grilled with the same old bottled barbecue sauce. This is another way of cooking chicken—with lime and herbs, which impart a fresh, original accent.

3 small broiler chickens, halved	LIME SAUCE ½ cup salad oil
¼ lb butter	½ cup fresh lime juice
1 Tbsp minced parsley	3 Tbsp chopped chives
1 tsp tarragon	½ tsp salt
1 tsp rosemary	½ tsp Tabasco sauce
3 tsp salt	

Wash and dry the chicken. Cream the butter with the minced parsley, tarragon, and rosemary. Loosen the breast skin on the chicken with a knife, insert the herb butter under the skin, and pat the skin back into place. Sprinkle chickens with 3 tsp salt. Combine the ingredients for the lime sauce and brush the mixture over the chickens. Place them on a greased barbecue grill over a slow coal fire, about 8 inches from the coals. Baste frequently with the lime sauce, turning every 10 minutes until golden brown, about 35 minutes.

Madam Butterfly Leg of Lamb

This leg of lamb, boned and "butterflied" by the butcher, grills to tender pink perfection on the inside in about 50 minutes, just time enough to savor a couple of drinks in the singing wilderness before dinner. While pink lamb is the only way to have it, if you insist on brown meat, plan on about 1 hour and 10 minutes. Either way, it's best to cut into the meat and check the desired color as you would for a steak. The marinade imparts a light Oriental accent, most honorable.

1 4-to-5-lb leg of lamb, boned and flattened for grill

MARINADE

6 oz Japanese soy sauce

½ cup dry sherry

grated rind and juice of 1 orange

2 cloves garlic, crushed

1 tsp ginger

Place the lamb in a large flat pan. Combine the marinade and pour over the lamb. Marinate for several hours before grilling. Grill 6 to 8 inches from the coals. Baste frequently and turn lamb every 7 or 8 minutes.

Sesame Spareribs

These ribs are neither Western, Polynesian, Oriental, nor Cliché. The principal flavor is sesame, an inspired seasoning with pork.

6 lb lean spareribs

MARINADE

½ cup salad oil
2 cups soy sauce

2 cloves garlic, crushed
3 tsp sugar
4 Tbsp crushed sesame
seeds

Preboil ribs for ½ hour to remove excess fat and shorten cooking time on the grill. Combine the marinade (mash the garlic and sesame seeds in a mortar with a pestle or with a wooden mallet), and pour marinade over meat. Let stand for several hours. Grill the ribs over low coals, basting frequently with marinade.

Charcoal-Broiled Shrimp

If you are camping near an ocean or gulf where you can buy fresh jumbo-sized shrimp or prawns, cook them this way. If you can't buy them ocean-fresh, at least get them in a fish market where they are packed in ice but not completely frozen, as they are in supermarkets. If possible, use a hinged hand grill. You can turn the shrimp over more easily; the hinged grill lies on top of the regular grill.

24 jumbo-sized shrimp or
prawns

24 anchovy fillets
12 slices lean bacon

Peel the shrimp or prawns. Split them deeply down the back, devein, and insert an anchovy fillet in each split. Cut the slices of lean bacon lengthwise. Wrap half a slice of bacon around each shrimp or prawn, securing with a toothpick. Grill over coals until bacon is crisp, about 5 minutes or less. Don't overcook or they will dry out.

His Fish

He just might hook a fish! Don't burst into tears—get him to clean it and then grill it this way. Whatever the fish, it'll taste like a prize catch.

1 whole 5- or 6-lb fish (big
enough to serve 6)
½ cup chopped fresh
mushrooms
½ cup chopped green onion
tops
¼ cup Parmesan cheese
¼ lb butter, melted
3 slices lemon
salt and pepper to taste

After he has cleaned and scaled his fish, stuff the cavity with a mixture of chopped mushrooms and chopped green onion tops. Sprinkle Parmesan cheese over the stuffing. Place the fish on a double layer of foil, pour ¼ lb of melted butter over the fish, and garnish with lemon slices and salt and pepper to taste. Fold the foil tightly over the fish and fold up the edges. Put the package with the fold side down on the barbecue grill about 6 inches from the coals, and cook about ½ hour to 40 minutes. The time depends on the exact weight of the fish. The fish is grilled 15 minutes on one side, turned over, and grilled 15 minutes or longer, on the other side. Open the foil after a ½ hour and check whether it is done.

If you want to be really elaborate you can make a sauce to serve with the fish. Here's a sour-cream sauce that can be stirred up in a minute.

SOUR-CREAM SAUCE

½ cup melted butter
½ cup sour cream
½ tsp onion salt
1 tsp dill weed

Combine all ingredients and stir over low heat until warm.

High Sierra Trout

First, catch a trout. If you're not an angler, go ahead and buy one, but be sure it is a fresh-fresh trout, not fresh frozen. Fresh trout are available in many fish markets; they are flown in from various trout farms and arrive packed in ice. The aroma of sizzling trout on the grill is one of the great culinary fragrances. Trout is a fish made to be savored in the wilderness. If you can't find any wilderness, at least choose a serene spot for your picnic.

Although fresh trout really needs no gilding, we supply an interesting basting sauce to try with this delicacy.

6 small trout, or 3 large ones	**¼ cup cider vinegar**
	2 Tbsp brown sugar
SAUCE	**1 ½ tsp salt**
2 Tbsp minced onion	**1 tsp paprika**
⅔ cup butter	**1 tsp Worcestershire sauce**
1 cup white wine	**¼ tsp pepper**

Sauté the minced onion in the butter for a few minutes. Add the rest of the ingredients and simmer 5 minutes until flavors blend. Brush the trout generously with the sauce and grill over low coals, basting constantly, until tender. Small trout take about 5 minutes on each side, larger trout about 8 minutes. Skewer the trout so you can flip them over easily.

Barbecued Eggplant

The grill does as much for vegetables as for meat or chicken when you steam them in foil without water, just seasonings. Wrap any of your favorite vegetables in foil, separately or in combinations, accenting them first with a dab of butter, salt, pepper, and herbs. Here's an intriguing way of grilling eggplant.

6 slices peeled eggplant, 1-inch thick	**6 Tbsp butter**
12 thin slices tomato	**2 tsp salt**
6 thin slices onion	**1 tsp pepper**
6 large mushroom caps, sliced	**1 tsp basil**
	1 tsp oregano

Cut 6 squares of foil sufficiently large to fold over vegetables combined in individual servings. Top each slice of eggplant with 2 thin slices tomato, 1 slice onion, 1 sliced mushroom cap, and 1 Tbsp of butter. Sprinkle each portion with salt, pepper, basil, and oregano. Fold foil over and seal airtight. Place on the grill and cook for about 15 minutes.

Texas Barbecue Sauce

The most famous barbecue hails from the Lone Star State. The secret is in the sauce. There are many imitations of this spicy sauce, but none has the flavor of the native product. Here it is—straight from a Texas chef who prepares Texas barbecues in Texas. Note there is no catsup in it.

1½ tsp salt
1½ tsp dry mustard
1 clove garlic, minced
½ tsp crumbled bay leaf
1 tsp chili powder
1½ tsp paprika
1 tsp Tabasco sauce

⅔ cup Worcestershire sauce
½ cup wine vinegar
2⅔ cups beef bouillion
⅓ cup salad oil
1½ tsp monosodium glutamate

Combine all ingredients and let blend overnight or for a couple of days.

This is a great basting sauce—or "mopping sauce," as the Texans put it—with all kinds of meat, but especially beef. Try it with steaks, also brisket of beef. Preboil the brisket for a couple of hours, until nearly tender, using the recipe for Boiled Brisket of Beef (see Index). Finish cooking the brisket, the last half hour or so, on the grill. Brush the meat lavishly with Texas Barbecue Sauce and baste frequently. You can preboil the brisket at home, if you like, and keep it wrapped in foil in the camper refrigerator until you are ready for the barbecue. It keeps beautifully for several days.

Hawaiian Teriyaki Sauce

Teriyaki is used as a marinade and basting sauce for a number of meats, especially shish kebabs. This version has a unique accent—bourbon. It comes by way of Hawaii, where it must have picked up a little Navy whisky; traditionally, Teriyaki is flavored with Japanese mirin wine.

8 oz Japanese soy sauce
2 oz bourbon
2 Tbsp sugar
1 Tbsp monosodium glutamate

1 Tbsp sesame oil
1 Tbsp powdered ginger, or 1 tsp grated fresh ginger
1 clove garlic, minced fine

Combine all ingredients. Marinate meat or fowl in the sauce for 2 or 3 hours before grilling. While grilling, baste frequently with the sauce.

Shelf Dinners

Crab Bisque

Homemade soup from a combination of cans. This thick, marvelous bisque, teamed with a salad and hot rolls, makes an appetizing lunch you can stir together in minutes.

2 cans tomato soup
2 cans pea soup
3 cups evaporated milk

2 6½-oz cans crabmeat
3 Tbsp dry sherry

Blend the tomato soup, pea soup, and evaporated milk. (This makes a thicker soup than the usual equal proportions of milk and soup). Drain the crabmeat, flake it, and remove shell bits. Add the crabmeat to the soup and stir in the sherry. Heat to boiling point, but do not boil.

Spaghetti with Wine Sauce

In Italy the movable feast never moves without a spaghetti pot. Freshly cooked pasta is always on the picnic menu. Try this beautiful spaghetti with wine sauce. It's different!

1 ¼ lb spaghetti
5 qts water
2 Tbsp salt
freshly grated Parmesan
cheese

SAUCE

1 red onion, sliced thin
5 Tbsp olive oil
2 Tbsp water

1 whole red chili pepper,
crushed
¾ lb bacon (canned bacon
can be used), cut in 1-inch
pieces
6 Tbsp dry white wine
1 1-lb-12-oz can Italian
plum tomatoes
1 tsp salt
1 tsp basil

To make the sauce, sauté the onion in the olive oil for 3 or 4 minutes. Add 2 Tbsp water and the crushed chili pepper and simmer for a few minutes. Add the bacon. When bacon is cooked (but still soft), pour off all but 4 Tbsp of the fat (leaving the chili pepper) and add the wine. Simmer 2 or 3 minutes, then add the plum tomatoes, salt, and basil. Simmer 5 minutes. Meanwhile put the spaghetti in a large pot containing 5 qts boiling water and 2 Tbsp salt. When the water returns to a boil, stir the spaghetti so it will not stick together and cook for 12 minutes or until it is chewy inside — al dente, as the Italians say. Never overcook any pasta—even another minute can ruin spaghetti and make it mushy. Drain the spaghetti in a colander, rinse quickly with cold water, and return to the pot. Reheat for a few seconds and pour the hot sauce over the spaghetti. Serve with freshly grated Parmesan cheese on the side.

Camper Stew

Stew traveled west with the pioneers and is still traveling in today's camper kitchens. There is nothing so satisfying after a long day on the freeway trail.

3 12-oz cans cooked roast
  beef with gravy
1 can beef bouillon
2 Tbsp flour
1 Tbsp onion flakes
1 tsp thyme
1 bay leaf
1 Tbsp parsley flakes

2 8½-oz cans mixed
  tiny peas and onions
2 8½-oz cans cooked
  carrots
1 15-oz can small cooked
  potatoes
salt and pepper to taste

Cut the cooked roast beef into stew-sized chunks. For this I prefer the canned beef imported from Argentina. Put the meat and gravy into a pot. Mix the beef bouillon with the flour and add. Bring to a simmer, then add the rest of the ingredients. Simmer slowly, stirring constantly, until meat and vegetables are hot. If you desire more gravy, increase the amount of beef bouillon.

Mexican Casserole

Mexican food lends itself to a variety of flavorful casseroles. Keep a supply of south-of-the-border specialties in your camper kitchen for improvised meals. This combination of chili beans and tamales can be fired up with as much Tabasco as you like.

2 15-oz cans chili con carne
Tabasco sauce to taste
2 15-oz cans tamales
2 7-oz cans corn niblets

1 cup shredded cheddar
  cheese
1 cup crushed corn chips

Season the chili con carne to taste with Tabasco and heat in a saucepan. Place the tamales on the bottom of a casserole; pour chile con carne over tamales. Drain the corn niblets, sprinkle over the beans, and top casserole with the shredded cheese. Sprinkle the crushed corn chips on top. Bake in a moderate oven (350°) until heated through, about 20 minutes.

Shelf Paella

This might not evoke *olés* from a Spaniard, but for a make-shift paella it is surprisingly tasty. All the ingredients are straight off the shelf with the exception of the chorizos (Mexican sausage), which keeps for weeks in a refrigerator. Try this on your boat too, or anywhere dinner starts with a can opener.

2 chorizos, skinned and cut in small pieces
¼ cup olive oil
1½ cups long-grain rice
1 7½-oz can minced clams
¼ cup clam juice from minced clams
2¾ cups chicken broth
1½ tsp salt
3 4½-oz cans shrimp, drained
1 small jar pimentos, cut in strips

Fry the skinned pieces of chorizo in the olive oil. Add the rice and stir until rice is golden brown. Add the minced clams and clam broth, the chicken broth, and the salt. Cover pot and cook slowly 10 minutes. Uncover and sprinkle the shrimp on top. Cover again and steam-cook another 5 minutes or so, until rice is tender but not mushy. Garnish with strips of pimento.

Chicken Divan from Cans

You'll be amazed at the culinary magic you can weave with canned chicken, canned asparagus, and canned chicken soup. This tastes just like Chicken Divan but contains asparagus instead of broccoli. It's a shelf picnic you'll make at home as well as on the road. Always use the best canned chicken available, even if it is more expensive. The dish demands it.

2 14½-oz cans green   1 cup mayonnaise
  asparagus spears   2 tsp lemon juice
2 11-oz cans sliced cooked   1 tsp curry powder
  chicken   ½ cup grated Parmesan
2 cans cream of chicken   cheese
  soup

Warm the asparagus spears in their liquid. Drain asparagus and arrange in greased baking dish. Lay the slices of cooked chicken over the asparagus. Combine in a bowl the cream of chicken soup, mayonnaise, lemon juice, and curry powder. Pour over chicken. Sprinkle top with grated Parmesan and bake for 30 minutes.

Spanish Rice with Shrimp

The flavored rice mixes are a boon to the camper chef. This recipe combines Spanish Rice mix with shrimp, cheese, and mushrooms.

1 6-oz package Spanish Rice 2 3-oz cans sliced mush-
  mix   rooms, drained
2 cups canned tomatoes   4 oz cheddar cheese, grated
2 Tbsp butter
3 4½-oz cans shrimp,
  drained

Cook the Spanish Rice mix with the canned tomatoes and butter according to package directions. When rice is almost tender, stir in the shrimp, mushrooms, and grated cheese. Stir constantly over low heat until cheese melts and shrimp and mushrooms are hot.

Maryland Crab Cakes

With little old Maryland crab cakes browned in your skillet and spoon bread on the side, you have a real Southern feast—from canned crab and spoon-bread mix.

2 7½-oz cans crabmeat   ½ cup breadcrumbs
1 egg, beaten   ½ cup flour
½ cup mayonnaise   2 eggs, beaten
2 Tbsp onion flakes   ½ cup breadcrumbs
1 Tbsp celery flakes   ¼ cup cooking oil
1 Tbsp Worcestershire sauce   1 box spoon-bread mix
1 Tbsp Rose's Lemon Juice

Drain the crabmeat and remove shell bits. Mix with 1 beaten egg, mayonnaise, onion flakes, celery flakes, Worcestershire sauce, Rose's Lemon Juice, and ½ cup breadcrumbs. Shape the mixture into 12 flat, round cakes. Dip each cake first into the flour, then into the 2 beaten eggs, then into ½ cup breadcrumbs. Heat the cooking oil in a skillet and brown cakes on both sides. The spoon-bread mix stirs up as simply as any mix, bakes in ½ hour, and is good enough to eat with a spoon!

CHAPTER VII

The Sportsman's Lunchbox

There are golf widows, bowling widows, fishing widows, hunting widows, and poker-game widows. Whatever kind you are — be brave! A husband's right to an occasional outing with the boys is an unwritten, iron-clad clause in every marriage contract.

If you can't join him, feed him. It's good for a lot of merit badges. Sportsmen's appetites are as untamed as the great outdoors. Pack a lunch keyed to masculine tastes. No dainty watercress sandwiches or pretty Waldorf salad. Curb your wifely instinct to count his calories or stuff him with sensible roughage. Let him enjoy the hearty, satisfying foods he really loves. This is *his* picnic.

What do men love? Meat, simply prepared and plentiful, for one thing. (They may be gourmets at home, but they're gourmands with the boys.) You can cook a variety of meats that slice up into thick, juicy sandwich fillings Choose a bread that's dark and zesty, a large-sized rye or pumpernickel that tastes marvelous slathered with sweet butter.

There's a little bit of Dagwood in every husband, so build him a sandwich of his favorite ingredients — meat, cheese, pickles, chili sauce, mustard, or whatever. Remember, a man invented the sandwich, and it's a male prerogative to have it in any indigestible combination he wants. (However, we offer some sandwich combinations he'll relish without the heartburn.)

Soups, both hot and cold, are welcome additions to the sportsman's lunchbox. In the shivering dawn of a duck blind, the mighty hunter husband will bless you for a thick, comforting potage. On the scorching deck of a fishing barge, a thermos of icy soup will cool his temper when the big one gets away.

Remember, of course, to fill the seemingly bottomless thermos of coffee and pack an energizing sweet of some kind, if only a few candy bars. And if you're really bucking for a Distinguished Service Cross, don't forget the beer!

Vichyssoise with Watercress

Nothing is colder than a cold potato, especially when it's chilled with watercress in a fabulous soup. He'll really bless you for pouring this green-flecked Vichyssoise into his thermos.

2 leeks, thoroughly cleaned and sliced	1 Tbsp salt
2 onions, chopped	2 cups milk
4 boiling potatoes, peeled and sliced	2 cups heavy cream
3 cups chicken broth	½ bunch watercress leaves, chopped

Combine the leeks, onions, and raw potato slices in a saucepan with the chicken broth and salt. Slowly simmer, covered, until vegetables are tender. Cool. Pour into blender and mix until puréed, about 2 to 3 minutes. Add the chopped watercress and blend another minute. Pour into a bowl, add the milk and heavy cream. Stir and chill.

Lentil Soup

All men love lentil soup is a generalization; there are probably a dozen men in the world who hate it. If he isn't among the dozen, make him a thermos of this rich, substantial potage. What a warming thought for the crack-of-dawn hunter!

12 oz lentils, washed and drained	1 tsp pepper
	½ tsp thyme
¼ lb bacon, diced	2 bay leaves
1 medium onion, chopped	6 bouillon cubes
1 cup diced carrots	1 large raw potato, peeled
2 qts water	1 large ham hock
1 cup chopped celery	2 Tbsp red wine vinegar
3 tsp salt	

Wash the lentils and soak overnight in cold water to cover. Drain. In a Dutch oven, sauté the diced bacon until fairly crisp. Add the onion and carrots and sauté until onions are golden. Add the lentils, 2 qts water, celery, salt, pepper, thyme, bay leaves, and bouillon cubes. Grate the raw potato into the soup. Add the ham hock and the wine vinegar. Simmer, covered, for 1½ hours. Remove the bay leaves and ham hock. Slice the meat off the ham hock, dice the meat, and return meat to the pot. Cover again and simmer another 15 minutes.

Ninth-Hole Soup

Mad dogs, Englishmen, and golfers go out in the noon-day sun. This icy tomato consommé for the ninth hole has a wee bracer of vodka — not enough to ruin his game, just enough to improve his temper.

3 12-oz cans tomato juice	6 Tbsp minced green pepper
3 13-oz cans consommé Madrilène	6 Tbsp lemon juice
	1 ½ tsp salt
6 Tbsp minced green onions	12 Tbsp vodka

Pour the tomato juice into a pitcher with the unchilled consommé Madrilène. Stir with 7 or 8 ice cubes until icy cold. Add the remaining ingredients and stir well. Correct seasoning to taste (you may want a little more salt or lemon) and pour into a wide-necked thermos. This is a liberal amount for a foursome, but this happy soup invites "seconds."

Jiggs' Special

A salute to Jiggs and Dinty Moore's! A luscious fresh corned beef sandwich with shredded cabbage. Don't forget the beer, Maggie!

6 Tbsp butter	3 Tbsp mayonnaise
3 tsp horseradish	6 slices homemade corned beef, cut ½ inch thick
12 slices rye bread from large-sized loaf	3 Tbsp Dijon mustard
1 ½ cups shredded cabbage	6 slices Swiss cheese

Blend the butter with horseradish and spread on the rye-bread slices. Blanch the shredded cabbage in boiling water until slightly wilted — a few minutes. Drain and mix with the mayonnaise. On 6 slices of the bread put the slices of corned beef and spread the meat with the mustard. Top each with 2 Tbsp shredded cabbage and a slice of Swiss cheese. Cover with the remaining bread slices. Cut sandwiches diagonally for easier eating. The cabbage must be kept between the corned beef and the cheese so the bread won't get soggy.

Smoked Salmon and Smoked Trout Sandwich

If you want to hook a compliment from an angler, put this lure in his lunchbox. It's an unusual triple-decker sandwich with smoked salmon in the bottom section and smoked trout in the top section.

18 slices whole-wheat bread, preferably coarse-grained	**½ tsp cayenne pepper**
8 Tbsp butter	**1 8-oz can Rainbow Smoked Trout**
6 slices smoked salmon	**2 Tbsp mayonnaise**
juice of ½ lemon	**2 Tbsp minced chives**

Spread all the slices of bread with butter. On each of 6 slices, put 1 slice smoked salmon (drained if you're using canned smoked salmon) and sprinkle with lemon juice. Season with cayenne pepper. Top salmon with another slice of bread, buttered side up. Mix the smoked trout with the mayonnaise and chives and spread on the second layer of bread in each sandwich. Top each with one of the remaining 6 slices of bread. Cut sandwiches in two crosswise.

Baked Bean Sandwich

Who would think of putting Boston baked beans in a sandwich? No proper Bostonian—it must have been a prospector. This sandwich is simple, substantial, and honest as beans.

1 1-lb-11-oz can Boston baked beans	**4 Tbsp chili sauce**
2 Tbsp grated sweet onion	**6 Tbsp butter**
	12 slices pumpernickel

Drain the beans, mash them with a fork, and add the grated sweet onion and chili sauce. Spread all the slices of pumpernickel generously with butter. Spread the bean mixture evenly on 6 slices and top with remaining slices.

Western Steak Sandwich

1 3-lb top sirloin cut 2 inches thick	6 Tbsp butter
salt and pepper to taste	12 Tbsp blue cheese
12 slices French bread or Sour Dough (large, circular loaf)	3 Tbsp Worcestershire sauce
	6 slices red onion

Season steak with salt and pepper and broil to medium rare. (The meat should be at least pink for the best flavor.) Trim off all fat and slice steak crosswise in ¼ inch strips. Lightly toast 12 slices of French bread or Sour Dough from the large-size loaf that gives you a big sandwich. Cream the butter with the blue cheese and Worcestershire sauce. Slather all 12 slices of the toasted bread with this spread. Arrange 4 or 5 steak strips on each of the 6 slices of bread, top each with a slice of red onion, and cover with remaining 6 slices of bread. Incidentally, this is a great recipe for leftover steak or any grilled or roasted meat.

The Closed Open-Face Sandwich

Close a Danish open-face sandwich and you have a traveling treat—especially this one, which has layers of sharp cheddar cheese and liverwurst, accented with anchovy and onion. It deserves the best moist and crusty rye bread you can find.

12 slices moist rye bread (large-sized loaf)	12 thin slices liverwurst
6 Tbsp butter	6 thin slices tomato
6 slices sharp cheddar cheese	12 anchovy fillets
	6 slices sweet red onion

Spread all 12 slices of bread with butter. On each of 6 slices, layer the following ingredients: 1 slice cheese, 2 slices liverwurst, 1 slice tomato, 2 anchovy fillets, and 1 slice onion. Cover with the remaining slices of bread and cut diagonally.

Shooter's Sandwich

This is a traditional picnic favorite of the "guns" (hunters) in Scotland and England. It has been said, "With this shooter's sandwich and a flask of whisky-and-water, a man may travel from Land's End to John O'Groats and snap his fingers at both." No wonder! It's made with a whole loaf of bread scooped out and filled with ground meat and herbs. Your hunter will love it—tradition and all.

1½-lb loaf day-old unsliced white bread	½ tsp pepper
⅛ lb butter	2 Tbsp chopped green onions
½ tsp thyme	1 tsp prepared mustard
½ tsp oregano	1 Tbsp Worcestershire sauce
1 Tbsp minced parsley	1 Tbsp tomato paste
1¼ lb ground round steak	½ tsp curry
1 tsp salt	1 egg, beaten
	2 Tbsp milk

It's best to get day-old white bread from a bakery. The weight doesn't have to be exact to the ounce, but the loaf must be big enough to accommodate the stuffing. Remove a 1-inch-thick slice from one end of the loaf and scoop out the inside, leaving a crust ¾ inch thick at top, bottom, and sides. Melt the butter and mix with the thyme, oregano, and parsley. Brush the inside of the loaf as well as the cut side of the end piece with the herb butter. Make breadcrumbs from the inside of the loaf and mix ½ cup of these with the meat, salt, pepper, green onions, mustard, Worcestershire sauce, tomato paste, curry, and beaten egg. Pack the meat mixture into the scooped-out loaf. Replace the sliced end and tie it in place with a string. Brush the outside with the milk and wrap the loaf loosely in greased foil. Bake in a moderate oven 1½ hours. Let cool at room temperature. Pack a knife with this sandwich to cut the string and slice.

Surfer's Submarine

This sub sandwich cruises with a full complement of meats, cheese, fish, hard-cooked eggs, relishes, and whatever else you want to put in it—delicatessen ammunition to torpedo the biggest appetite! Surfers and skin-divers, a notoriously famished brotherhood, really go for these robust foot-long sandwiches. Here's a way of building a sub that is a favorite with the California beach crowd. The recipe is based on one sandwich for one person; if you are launching a fleet of subs, multiply.

12 inches French bread (buy a long crusty loaf and slice it off)	**4 slices bologna**
	4 slices Swiss cheese
	6 slices cucumber
4 Tbsp whipped butter seasoned with ½ tsp garlic powder	**½ green pepper, seeded and sliced in strips**
	½ tsp basil
4 slices Italian salami	**½ tsp salt**

Cut the 12-inch piece French bread in half lengthwise and slather with the seasoned butter. Cut the slices of Italian salami, bologna, and Swiss cheese in half and spread the halves out on half the bread so that the meats and cheese overlap and cover the surface. Top with the slices of cucumber and strips of green pepper. Sprinkle with basil and salt. Cover with remaining half of bread. Wrap the whole sandwich in foil.

Hunter's Hamburger

This is a muscular sandwich for rugged appetites. Its secret—baked beans in the heart of the burger. Are broiled hamburgers good cold? Yes, if the roll is toasted and spread lavishly with butter seasoned with parsley or chives.

1½ lb ground round steak
1½ tsp pepper
1 Tbsp Worcestershire sauce
¼ tsp pepper
1 Tbsp ice water
6 heaping Tbsp brown baked beans

6 hard rolls
6 Tbsp butter
6 tsp chopped parsley or chives

Mix the meat with the salt, Worcestershire sauce, pepper, and ice water. Form into 12 patties and put 1 heaping Tbsp brown baked beans on top of each of 6 patties. Cover with remaining 6 patties, pressing edges together. Broil to individual taste. Split and toast the rolls, spread with butter seasoned with chopped parsley or chives, and put in the hamburgers.

Poker Player's Peanut Butter

The peanut-butter sandwich that goes to the poker game with the boys has to be nourishing—this is a strenuous sport. It also has to be man-sized and lusty. This poker-game picnic special provides enough for the gang.

1 6-oz jar crunchy peanut butter
6 thick slices bologna

1 large sweet red onion, sliced
12 slices pumpernickel

Spread peanut butter on all 12 slices of pumpernickel and top 6 slices with a thick slice of bologna and 1 slice of sweet red onion. Cover with remaining bread, making 6 sandwiches with bologna and onion in the middle of each.

Fisherman's Tuna Sandwich

Two popular sandwich fillings blended into one wonderful lunchbox treat. The lively seasonings give it a grownup taste.

1 6½-oz can white tuna
1 cup diced Swiss cheese
½ cup chopped green pepper
⅓ cup mayonnaise (or more)

1 tsp onion salt
½ tsp dill weed
1 tsp lemon juice
12 slices whole-wheat bread

Drain and flake the tuna and combine with the cheese and green pepper. Blend the mayonnaise with the onion salt, dill weed, and lemon juice. Mix with the tuna and cheese. Spread filling generously on 6 slices grainy-textured wheat bread and top with remaining slices.

Boiled Brisket of Beef

This is a brown, rich, savory meat that men love—and women seldom cook. Popular in Europe, boiled brisket of beef in this country is usually found only in delicatessens. We urge you to try this versatile meat; it is inexpensive and excellent for cold cuts, sandwiches, and meat salads. If you can boil water, this is your dish. All it takes is 2 or 3 hours' simmering. It's an inspired sandwich filling for the kids' lunchbox, too.

4-lb lean brisket of beef
1 tsp salt
1 tsp pepper
1 tsp rosemary or thyme
1 onion stuck with 2 cloves
3 leeks, coarsely chopped

3 carrots, coarsely chopped
1 rib celery, chopped
1 sprig parsley
1 heaping Tbsp salt
4 Tbsp butter (optional)

Rub the brisket with 1 tsp salt, the pepper, and the rosemary or thyme. Place it in a large pot, together with the flavoring vegetables: the onion stuck with cloves, the leeks, carrots, celery, and parsley. Add sufficient water barely to cover meat and bring to a boil for 5 minutes. Skim off surface foam from stock, add 1 heaping Tbsp salt, reduce heat, cover pot, and simmer for 2½ to 3 hours — until meat is fork-tender. Remove brisket from pot and quickly brown in the butter in a skillet. (This last step is optional; it gives the brisket a rich brown color on the outside. But the meat is equally tasty straight from the pot.) When you make this into sandwiches, add a dab of horseradish or mustard to the beef. And why not a slice of red onion?

Homemade Corned Beef

Another sandwich meat that has to come fresh and juicy from the pot to be relished. Canned corned beef bears little resemblance to the homemade, petal pink, succulent variety. In addition to making a sandwich filling, corned beef can be used for dinner, youngsters' lunches, and the inevitable stew. All these meats are so versatile and practical, they're well worth the time to prepare. To allow for shrinkage, buy a generous-sized brisket.

4-lb corned brisket of beef	**2 carrots, chopped**
6 peppercorns	**1 large onion, chopped**
1 bay leaf	**2 turnips, sliced**
½ cup brown sugar	

Trim off any excess fat from the corned beef and put it in a good-sized pot with enough cold water to cover. Cover pot and bring to a simmer slowly. Skim off surface foam. Add the peppercorns, bay leaf, and brown sugar (the sugar is a very special added touch of flavor). Cover and cook slowly for 2½ hours. Then add, for flavoring only, the carrots, onion, and turnips. Cover and simmer for another hour or so — until meat is tender. Pour off half the cooking water and let the meat cool in the remaining water. Remove and press brisket with a weight, for half an hour, to retain its shape. Keep wrapped in foil to retain juices and flavor. Corned beef keeps beautifully in the refrigerator. Don't overlook this for family picnics, sliced and served cold with mustard.

German Potato Salad

This substantial salad is worth its weight in calories.

6 **medium-sized boiling po-**
  tatoes
1½ **tsp sugar**
1 **tsp salt**
1 **tsp dry mustard**

¼ **tsp ground black pepper**
3 **Tbsp white vinegar**
1 **cup sour cream**
2 **Tbsp chopped chives**

Peel the potatoes and boil them whole, until cooked but still firm. Mushy potatoes ruin this dish. While the potatoes are still warm, cut them in ½-inch slices. In a bowl, mix the sugar, salt, dry mustard, pepper, and vinegar. Stir in the sour cream, then pour the dressing over the potatoes. Toss lightly until potatoes are coated and sprinkle with chopped chives. This is one of those flexible dishes, good hot or cold.

Next-Day Meatloaf

There's a trick to this recipe: try to save enough meatloaf for sandwiches the next day. Chances are it will be demolished by midnight refrigerator-raiders. This and the following meatloaf make moist, plump sandwiches that men love —also women, children, and all picnickers.

1½ lb ground round steak
¾ lb pork sausage
½ cup cottage cheese
½ cup dry breadcrumbs
¼ cup chili sauce
½ cup chopped onions
2 eggs, beaten

1 Tbsp chopped green
   pepper
1 Tbsp chopped parsley
1½ tsp salt
½ tsp pepper
3 hard-cooked eggs

Combine the ground round steak with all the other ingredients except the hard-cooked eggs. Line a greased 9- by 5- by 3-inch loaf pan with waxed paper and pack half of the meat into the pan. Place the whole hard-cooked eggs lengthwise on the center of the meat and cover with the remaining meat mixture. Chill 1 hour. Unmold the loaf into a roasting pan, removing the waxed paper. Bake at 350° for 1 hour to 1 hour and 15 minutes. Each slice of meat will have a slice of egg in its center.

Cheddar Meatloaf

1 large sweet red pepper
4 Tbsp chopped red onion
3 Tbsp butter
1½ lb ground round steak
2 cups crumbled Saltines
1½ tsp salt
½ tsp paprika

½ tsp pepper
½ tsp Tabasco sauce
2 eggs, beaten
1 cup milk
½ lb diced cheddar cheese
1 Tbsp butter

Remove the stem and seeds from the red pepper, slice from it 6 thin rings, and save these for topping. Chop the remaining red pepper and saute with the red onion in the 3 Tbsp butter. Combine with the ground round steak, Saltines, salt, paprika, pepper, Tabasco sauce, beaten eggs, and milk. Mix well and add the cheddar cheese. Grease a meatloaf pan, line it with greased foil, and pack the mixture into it. Sauté the red-pepper rings in 1 Tbsp butter and decorate top of loaf. Bake 1 hour.

Ski Picnics

Ski widows are rare. This is a sport where wives are welcome, especially if they know how to pack a nifty knapsack ski picnic. Ski-hut snack bars are usually available at the top of the slopes, but invariably the food is dreary and conditions crowded. You'll do better to tote your own picnic: a big thermos of warming soup, hearty sandwiches, stuffed eggs, cheese and—if you like—a split of wine you can chill in the snow. Carry as much as you need up the ski lift—you'll be zooming down with a light knapsack.

Ski Soup

Here's a lusty ham-garbanzo soup that's a skier's delight. Have it on the slopes or at the end of the day when you're thawing out in front of the fire. If you have your own cabin, make a big potful; it disappears fast. If you want to stretch it, add another can of tomatoes or beans. It's that kind of soup, easy to get along with.

1 **ham bone**
½ **lb chopped ham (from a shank end of a baked ham)**
1 **large onion, chopped**
2 **carrots, sliced**
3 **Tbsp chopped parsley**
½ **tsp basil**
½ **tsp oregano**
1 **Tbsp salt**
1 **tsp pepper**
1 **1-lb can tomatoes**
1 **cup dry white wine**
5 **cups beef bouillon**
1 **cup diced uncooked potatoes**
1 **14-oz can of garbanzos (chick peas)**

Combine all the ingredients in a large pot and simmer for 20 minutes or longer. Be sure to cut vegetables small enough to go into a wide-necked thermos. For the slopes, take along thermos cups, spoons, and French bread.

Pistou Soup

Another robust soup you'll savor when you're wearing damp boots and a frost-bitten nose. Pistou is a remarkable French soup with zesty seasoning.

1 cup diced onions	2 tsp salt
1 leek (white part only), washed thoroughly and sliced	1 tsp pepper
	2 cloves garlic
	2 tsp basil
2 Tbsp butter	1 tsp thyme
1 cup fresh green beans cut into ½-inch lengths	½ tsp sage
	2 egg yolks
1 cup diced potatoes	¼ cup olive oil
1 cup canned tomatoes	2 Tbsp tomato paste
6 cups beef bouillon	2 Tbsp freshly grated
½ cup vermicelli broken into 1-inch lengths	Parmesan cheese

Sauté the onions and the white part of the leek in the butter until soft and tender. Transfer to a pot with a cover. Add the green beans, potatoes, canned tomatoes, and beef bouillon. Cover and simmer gently for 30 minutes, or until the vegetables are cooked. Add the salt, pepper, and vermicelli, and cook 15 minutes longer. In a bowl, mash the garlic with the basil, thyme, and sage. Add the egg yolks and gradually stir in the olive oil and tomato paste. Add a little soup to this mixture and stir back into the soup. Sprinkle with grated Parmesan cheese. Don't forget the spoons and thermos cups—this is a thick soup.

CHAPTER VIII

Motel Breakfasts

While a motel is hardly a Thoreau setting, room picnics have a touch of the gypsy that's fun. Moreover, they afford families economical and convenient dining. The simplest family breakfast in a coffee shop totals up to a sizable sum. And for what? Food so uniformly dreary it must be manufactured in a central kitchen in Kansas. How else can you explain the identical cup of bad coffee and rubbery eggs from coast to coast?

Breakfast, fortunately, is one meal that's easily brought from home or picked up en route and cooked on a portable burner in your room (as long as there's no state law prohibiting it). Many motels provide kitchenettes, which of course are the ultimate in convenience.

Motel picnics are as simple as a hard-cooked egg or as festive as fried chicken from the hamper. This is a meal where anything goes — from soup to dessert. Fruit pie, for example, is surprisingly tasty at sun-up. What could be more of a holiday for the youngsters than dessert the first thing in the morning? It may not be character-building, Mother, but it's fun!

The best motel breakfast starts in your own kitchen with homemade treats prepared the day of departure or the night before. With thermal equipment, foods stay fresh for 48 hours or longer. Often, however, it's more convenient to pick up snacks en route, from the grocery store, delicatessen, or bakery. These can also be appetizing, with a little touch of imagination or effort. (The effort may be as simple as heating a coffee cake and serving it with whipped sweet butter.) Whatever it is, it will be infinitely more satisfying and cheaper than a coffee-shop breakfast.

Consider, too, the advantage of brewing your own coffee. Coffee is the better half of breakfast. To some it *is* breakfast. Bring that essential eye-opener and soul-soother, an electric percolator, or a regular percolator and one-burner portable stove, and make proper coffee. Even your favorite instant is better than the "cuppa java" on the road; also, many motels have provisions for making instant coffee in your room. Incidentally, an especially pleasant breakfast coffee is café au lait, which is made with half hot milk and half strong coffee. For the youngsters, pack a thermos of hot cocoa or their favorite chocolate milk.

Today there are a number of cooking or heating units made expressly for traveling; some are listed in "Picnic Accessories" (see Index). However, one of the handiest items you can take is an electric popcorn popper, which doubles as a roomy pot to heat soups, stews, and other foods. Since the pot sits a little above the heating element, corn poppers warm food slowly without burning and also permit steaming. For frying as well as warming, or for making toast, an electric skillet is ideal.

Motel breakfasts require efficient execution from cooking to clean-up, but the advantages far outweigh the trouble.

Buttermilk Chicken

Let's start with a few homemade breakfasts to put in the hamper. Nothing could be more fun than fried chicken. This one is a version of Southern Fried Chicken, cooked without the skin. It's crispy and delectable. The buttermilk marinade gives it an original flavor. Wrap it in foil as soon as it is cooked to retain the moisture.

2 frying chickens, cut in serving pieces
1 qt buttermilk
2 cups flour, seasoned with salt and pepper
4 cups cooking oil
1 Tbsp salt

Remove skin from chicken parts and marinate the chicken in buttermilk for several hours, turning the pieces frequently. When you are ready to cook, dip chicken pieces in seasoned flour. Pour 2 cups of cooking oil in each of two skillets, and heat the oil until it is hot enough to sizzle when tested with a drop of water. Add the chicken and cook until golden brown and tender, about 20 minutes. Season chicken with the salt as it cooks. (The amount of salt really depends on your taste, but please don't underseason chicken.)

Gourmet Apple Pie

This is an apple pie you can't buy. It has a unique touch of peach jam and grated lemon rind and an honest-to-goodness crust.

2 cups flour
4 egg yolks, lightly beaten
4 Tbsp shortening
5 Tbsp white sugar
pinch of salt
1 egg, beaten
7 apples
2 tsp lemon juice
grated rind of 1 lemon
3 Tbsp peach jam
2 Tbsp brown sugar
2 tsp cinnamon

Put the flour in a mixing bowl with the lightly beaten egg yolks, shortening, sugar, and a pinch of salt. Stir and knead into a smooth, blended dough. Roll out ⅛ inch thick on a floured board and cut in half. Line a greased pie plate with half the pastry and brush the edges with the beaten egg. Peel, core, and slice the apples and combine with the lemon juice, lemon rind, peach jam, and brown sugar. Stir and pour into the lined pie plate. Sprinkle with cinnamon. Cover pie with top crust, prick several places with a fork, and brush with the remainder of the beaten egg. Bake until golden brown, about 40 minutes. Serve this lovely pie with café au lait.

Baked Stuffed Apples

This baked apple is an old friend of the family. It's sweet enough to be a dessert to the youngsters, nutritious enough to satisfy Mama, and hearty enough for Father. Try it for breakfast stuffed with chopped dates and walnuts and served with fresh cream or a dash of whipped cream (from the can).

6 red Roman Beauty apples	½ cup brown sugar
(or other large red apples)	½ cup water
½ cup chopped walnuts	6 Tbsp butter
½ cup chopped dates	3 tsp cinnamon

Core the apples and cut the bottoms to level them. Mix the chopped walnuts, chopped dates, brown sugar, and ¼ cup water. Fill the apples with the mixture. Dot each apple with 1 Tbsp butter and dust the apples with cinnamon. Pour the remaining ¼ cup water in the bottom of a buttered baking dish, place apples in dish, and bake about 45 minutes, or until apples are firm but cooked. Cool and transfer to a portable container.

Cream of Onion Soup

Onion soup served in a Paris market place at dawn makes an exciting breakfast, but, romantic tradition aside, you don't have to rise with the roosters to enjoy it. Onion soup warms the spirits any hour of the morning. So sleep in, and pour this breakfast soup from the thermos when you're ready to rise. Heat in a pot and serve. This is a variation of traditional onion soup, topped with crouton toast and flavored with a touch of apple. Make the toast at home and wrap in foil.

4 cans beef consommé **2 cups heavy cream**
3 onions, grated **salt to taste**
1 apple, peeled and grated

Pour the consommé and 1 can of water into a saucepan and add the grated onions and grated apple. Simmer in a covered pot until onions and apple are tender and have had time to flavor the consommé, about 15 or 20 minutes. Add the heavy cream and salt to taste and heat until cream is hot.

Crouton Toast

6 very thin slices French **1 can beef consommé**
bread

Cut 6 thin slices from a long narrow loaf of French bread. Dip each slice quickly into consommé — do not saturate. Place slices on a buttered cookie sheet and bake in a 250° oven until lightly browned. Turn with a spatula and brown on other side.

Orange Muffins

Feathery muffins with the good morning taste of orange juice. And so light! Serve them with peeled, sliced oranges marinated in French dressing.

2 cups sifted pastry flour	2 eggs, separated
3 Tbsp sugar	¾ cup orange juice
3 tsp baking powder	grated rind of 1 orange
1 tsp salt	¼ cup melted butter

Sift the flour with the sugar, baking powder, and salt. Beat the egg yolks until light and fluffy and add the orange juice and orange rind. Combine with the dry ingredients and mix well. Add the melted butter and beat well. Beat the egg whites until fluffy and fold them into the batter. Fill well-greased muffin cups two-thirds full to allow for rising. Bake in hot oven (425°) for about 15 minutes.

Blueberry Coffee Cake

Wait until you pluck this homemade blueberry coffee cake from the picnic hamper, and see how fast you rouse your family for breakfast. It's a real eye-opener!

2 cups sifted flour	1 egg
2 tsp baking powder	½ cup milk
½ tsp salt	2 cups canned blueberries,
¼ cup butter	drained
¾ cup sugar	

CRUMB TOPPING

½ cup sugar	½ tsp cinnamon
¼ cup flour	¼ cup butter

Sift 2 cups flour with the baking powder and salt. Cream ¼ cup butter and gradually beat in ¾ cup sugar. Add the whole egg and the milk and beat. Add to dry ingredients. Fold the blueberries into the batter. Spread batter in a greased and floured 8-inch square pan. To make the crumb topping, mix ½ cup sugar, ¼ cup flour, and the cinnamon. Cut in ¼ cup butter to form coarse crumbs. Sprinkle topping over the batter in the pan. Bake in a 375° oven for 40 to 45 minutes.

Honey French Toast

You've had French toast, but have you had it *this* way? Honey makes the delectable difference. We like it with orange honey, but you can use clover honey if you prefer. Bring the ingredients with you, the liquids mixed and ready to use.

2 eggs, slightly beaten
¼ cup milk
¼ cup honey
¼ tsp salt
6 to 8 slices white bread
3 Tbsp butter

Honey Sauce

1 cup honey
2 Tbsp lemon juice
2 Tbsp butter

Combine the beaten eggs, milk, ¼ cup honey, and salt. Dip the bread slices in the mixture and fry in butter until golden brown. To make the sauce, combine the ingredients (this can be done at home), heat, and serve over Honey French Toast.

Breakfast Blintzes

Here's a blintz as quick and easy to make as a sandwich. In fact, it's made from sandwich bread, which gives it a lighter, more delicate texture than that of the standard blintz. This bread casing can also be used for potato and fruit blintzes. It may not be kosher, but it's great!

24 slices soft white sandwich bread
1 pint small-cured cottage cheese
1 egg yolk, beaten
2 tsp soft butter
2 tsp vanilla extract or grated lemon rind
5 Tbsp butter
3 tsp cinnamon
1 cup sour cream

Cut crusts from the bread. Flatten each slice with a rolling pin until it is about ⅛ inch thick. Combine the cottage cheese with the beaten egg yolk, 2 tsp soft butter, and the vanilla extract or lemon rind (depending on whether you like a sweet or tart accent). Wrap the slices of bread casing in foil and put the cottage-cheese filling in a food thermos or insulated container. When you're ready to assemble the blintzes in the motel room, put 1 generous Tbsp of cottage-cheese mixture on each slice of bread and roll up the bread jelly-roll fashion, securing each blintz with a toothpick. Melt 5 Tbsp of butter in a skillet and sauté blintzes until golden brown, about 3 minutes. Keep turning them as you saute. Sprinkle with cinnamon and serve with sour cream on the side for a topping.

Quiche Lorraine

Quiche Lorraine puts breakfast in a pie! It combines the traditional bacon and eggs with Swiss cheese in a custard. As with the Salmon Quiche (see Index), this Gallic delight is delectable hot, hours from the stove, or served cold the next day.

1 **package piecrust mix**	¼ **tsp nutmeg**
½ **lb bacon, cut in 1-inch pieces**	½ **tsp salt**
	¼ **tsp cayenne pepper**
¾ **lb Swiss cheese, sliced**	1¼ **cup heavy cream**
4 **eggs**	

Make pastry as directed on package and line a 9-inch greased pie pan. Fry the bacon pieces until cooked but still soft. Drain. Spread a few slices of Swiss cheese on the pastry in the pie pan and sprinkle a few pieces of bacon over the cheese. Repeat layers of cheese and bacon, ending with cheese. Beat the eggs with the nutmeg, salt, and cayenne pepper. Pour in the heavy cream and pour the mixture over cheese-bacon layers. Bake pie at 375° for 35 or 40 minutes, or until golden brown on top. As with the Salmon Quiche, the soufflé puff will flatten as it cools, but the quiche will still be delicious for breakfast the next morning. Keep it tightly wrapped in foil.

Pick-up Picnics

The following are suggestions for breakfast picnics you can pick up in the grocery store, delicatessen, or bakery.

Avocado Stuffed with Mandarin Oranges

Nothing could be simpler than cutting an avocado in two, removing the pit, and filling the cavity with a few sections of mandarin oranges. However, it has a brilliant taste. Try a squeeze of lemon on top.

Hard-Cooked Eggs

Hard-cooked eggs are simple, basic, and nourishing. They can be made less simple and more interesting by adding a sprinkle of toasted onion flakes or a few dashes of Tabasco sauce; or buttering them with ham spread.

Breakfast Bagels

Bagels are as heavy as a bride's biscuits, but that's part of their solid charm. These substantial rolls with an old-country flavor make great eating in the morning when toasted, slathered with cream cheese, and topped with smoked salmon. The best ones are found in Jewish bakeries or grocery stores.

Fried Tomatoes and Brown-and-Serve Sausages

An easy and different breakfast that youngsters love (especially the egg-haters). Fry tomato slices in butter and sprinkle with basil. The brown-and-serve sausages are ready in minutes.

Orange Toast

In an electric skillet, sauté white bread in lots of bubbly butter until golden brown on both sides. Spread with a good English marmalade. Splurge a little on the marmalade. Fine jam adds elegance to breakfast.

Coffee Cake

Look with a wary eye on those ersatz coffee cakes with the gooey white icings that line the grocery shelves. The best coffee cakes are fresh from a bakery or found in the frozen food section. Wrap in foil, heat in an electric skillet, and serve with whipped butter, salt or sweet.

Fried Pineapple with Deviled Ham

Fresh pineapple is a luscious breakfast by itself, but canned pineapple needs adornment. Fry pineapple on one side in butter and top with a little deviled ham mixed with mayonnaise. Put the unfried side down in the skillet and cover pan. Fry just long enough to heat ham, 1 minute or less. If you have an oven, run the pineapple under the broiler. You'd be surprised how good this is.

Cream Cheese on Date-Nut Bread

A tea-hour classic that's equally appetizing in the morning. With a perfectly brewed pot of coffee or tea, it sums up the pleasure of a simple breakfast.

Creamed Chipped Beef on English Muffins

Mushroom soup plus canned mushrooms plus chipped beef equals a remarkably delicious creamed chipped beef to pour over toasted English muffins. Thin it with cream to the consistency you desire.

Spam Cakes

Another easy breakfast you can cook as quickly as you can say brush-your-teeth-wash-your-face-comb-your-hair-break-fast-is-ready. Make pancakes from a prepared liquid batter found in the frozen food section, stir in a can of Spam spread, and you're ready to pour some flavorful pancakes.

Brioches and Croissants

Venture away from the standard breakfast rolls and try croissants or brioches, the flaky, buttery French rolls that are a traditional part of a continental breakfast. Heat them and serve with a little whipped honey. You can usually buy croissants or brioches in bakeries as well as in the frozen food section of markets.

Rabbit Toast

The next best thing to a real Welsh rabbit is a makeshift Welsh rabbit. Toast an English muffin, spread with cheddar cheese soup (undiluted), and warm in a covered skillet until the cheese bubbles; to prevent burning, heat the muffins in an aluminum pie plate that fits inside the skillet. These plates are available in markets. You may also run the muffins under a broiler if one is available.

Cheese and Ham Biscuits

Buy a package of refrigerated biscuits, open, and insert small slices of American cheese and slices of ham between the layers of dough. Bake in a covered electric skillet 400° for 15 minutes or until biscuits are brown. Place biscuits in aluminum pie plate to prevent burning.

Smoked Kippered Herring and Smoked Whitefish

Anyone who has relished an English breakfast knows the delight of a good smoked kippered herring. Another savory treat for breakfast is smoked whitefish, which you can buy in Jewish groceries. It has the delicacy of trout and is delicious cold with a squeeze of lemon.

CHAPTER IX

Blithe Spirits

There's no happier place to toast Bacchus than wooded vale, sparkling shore, or any paradise that isn't posted. An idyllic setting makes beautiful wines more beautiful, "the adequate little wine" a real discovery.

Picnic wines range from the dry, light-bodied reds to the dry and medium-dry whites that uncork a mellow, fruity flavor. The latter wines often have a slight, subtle sweetness that complements cold dishes and the sunlit hour. Some people relish the more robust wines, such as burgundy or chianti, for picnic dining; but they afflict me with a dormouse drowsiness when imbibed at midday. At the end of this chapter we list some lilting picnic wines to pack in your hamper or cooler. Incidentally, we'd like to put in a kind word for the jug or gallon wine. Many of these inexpensive bulk wines are remarkably good and certainly appropriate to go to a picnic.

As for stronger spirits, the short, lethal cocktail has no place in paradise. Long, flavored drinks are more timely for the hour and the occasion.

Pre–Picnic Drinks

To launch your picnic, here's a bevy of beautiful drinks that toast the joy of the day. With wine on the menu, one drink is sufficient. Proportions are for one person. Multiply by the number of guests. With picnic drinks, it is wise to measure the liquor conservatively.

Rum Julep

2 oz light rum
1 tsp sugar
4 oz fresh lime juice

1 tsp fresh chopped mint
mint sprigs

In a blender, combine the rum, sugar, lime juice, chopped mint, and cracked ice. Blend for 10 seconds, then strain into thermos or pitcher to be kept chilled in the refrigerator. Serve with a sprig of fresh mint tucked in the glass.

Bull Shot

2 oz vodka
4 oz beef bouillon
1 tsp lemon juice

dash Worcestershire sauce
dash Tabasco sauce
(optional)

Combine the vodka, beef bouillon, lemon juice, and Worcestershire sauce in a cocktail pitcher. Add 5 or 6 ice cubes and stir for a minute until well chilled. Some people, but not all, like this with a dash of Tabasco; pass Tabasco separately when you serve the drinks.

Paradise Punch

2 oz dark rum
3 oz milk
3 oz half-and-half

1 heaping Tbsp Coconut
Snow (or any powdered
coconut for drinks)
sprinkle of nutmeg

In a blender or shaker, combine the rum, milk, half-and-half, and Coconut Snow or similar powdered coconut. Add 1 cup cracked ice and stir for a minute. Strain out ice and pour the punch into a thermos to keep icy cold. Just before serving, sprinkle with a shake of nutmeg.

Peach Champagne

1 oz chilled peach juice   **5 oz dry champagne**

The strained peach juice and champagne are carried separately to the picnic and combined in a chilled glass just before serving. The following recipe for peach juice will serve 6 to 8.

Peach Juice

8 very ripe peaches   **juice of 2 lemons**

Remove stones from peaches and press peaches through a sieve until only the skin remains. Add the lemon juice, pour into a container, and keep refrigerated.

Acapulco

½ oz Cointreau   **juice ½ lime**
1½ oz tequila   **4 oz pineapple juice**

Combine the ingredients in a shaker. Shake with cracked ice.

Appetizers

Appetizers aren't necessary on a picnic, but they're always welcome when you are serving drinks. This is the time to try new and provocative hors d'oeuvres, such as this Hungarian Cheese Spread.

Hungarian Cheese Spread

8 oz cream cheese
2 Tbsp whipped sweet butter
1 Tbsp finely chopped green pepper
1 Tbsp chopped chives

2 tsp chopped capers
¼ tsp dry mustard
¼ tsp salt
¼ tsp pepper
1 tsp Hungarian paprika

Mix the cream cheese with the whipped sweet butter. Blend in all the other ingredients. Shape into a mound and chill. Serve with thinly sliced pumpernickel.

Mushroom Pâté

1 4½-oz can Sell's Liver Paste (or other good liver paste)
4 oz cream cheese, softened
6 small mushrooms, chopped fine

1 clove garlic, minced
2 Tbsp butter
1 Tbsp dry sherry
½ tsp salt
¼ tsp pepper

Blend the liver paste with the softened cream cheese. Sauté the mushrooms and garlic in the butter for a minute or two and add to the cream cheese-liver paste mixture. Season with dry sherry, salt, and pepper. Refrigerate for several hours or until the mixture is fairly firm or has a pâté consistency.

Stuffed Raw Mushrooms

Wait until you discover how delicious mushrooms are before they're cooked—their flavor is even more exotic!

18 medium-sized mushroom caps

8 oz cream cheese

1 2½-oz can deviled ham

1 Tbsp Worcestershire sauce

Wash the mushroom caps (use only fresh, firm mushrooms). Blend the cream cheese with the deviled ham and Worcestershire sauce. Fill the raw mushroom caps with this mixture.

Hollandaise Stuffed Eggs

6 hard-cooked eggs

6 Tbsp whipped sweet butter

3 tsp lemon juice

salt to taste

Peel the hard-cooked eggs and cut in half. Scoop out the yolks and mash with the whipped sweet butter, lemon juice, and salt to taste. Spoon the mixture into the egg-white cavities.

Italian Salami Rolls

18 slices Italian salami

2 3¾-oz cans boneless, skinless sardines

9 green onions, chopped fine

2 Tbsp mayonnaise

1 Tbsp lemon juice

Remove outside skin from the slices of salami. Drain the sardines, mash, and combine with the green onions, mayonnaise, and lemon juice. Put 1 heaping tsp of the sardine mixture in the center of each slice of salami and roll it up, fastening with a toothpick.

Picnic Wines

And now to "wine that maketh glad the heart of man" — and maketh the picnic!

We must preface our list of picnic wines by saying that we are not connoisseurs of the grape in the true sense of the word. In this day and age of winemanship, this is a rare statement to make. We readily confess that we can't sip a wine, roll it on our tongue, and give its name, country of origin, vintage, vintner, and section of the vineyard from whence it came. We only know — as you do — that a good wine is self-evident and pleasing from the first sip to the last. Expensive or modestly priced, what really counts is not the label on the bottle, but the flavor of the grape and whether it pleases you. Wine is as personal as art. Like art, it is more fully appreciated with a little knowledge. The greater your familiarity with wines, the greater your enjoyment. So experiment. It's not expensive if you shop wisely for the good buys that are always available.

As for the color of the grape you serve, the choice really is yours; often, it depends on the richness or delicacy of the dish. No longer are there any firm rules about serving red wine with meat, white with poultry. Some subtle meats, such as veal, are better complemented by a chilled white wine or rosé than a red, and game such as wild duck takes on a red wine in style. Fish and shellfish, however, still are most often accompanied by a chilled white wine, not for tradition's sake alone but because it complements the delicacy of seafood.

Naturally, the "important" wines of France are outstanding in taste as well as price. The unimportant wines of France can also be excellent. Some of them are poor. This is the price of experimentation. There are also scores of fine German and Italian wines that are worth trying, and, happily enough, most of them are not too expensive.

For the price, of course, California wines are consistently the best. Price aside, some dazzling wines produced in California are the equal of any good Europeon wine. We're thinking especially of two of our favorite grapes, the red Cabernet Sauvignon and the white Chardonnay. New York State, which is the second most important wine-producing state after California, also offers a fine selection of American wines and is particularly noted for its excellent champagnes.

To give you as wide a choice as possible, we havé listed the best light-bodied red and white wines from France, Germany, Italy, California, and New York State. Also, there are suggestions for specific wines to serve with the wine-inspiring dishes throughout the book. You will note many mellow, fruity, slightly sweet wines on the list. As we mentioned, these wines are especially suited to picnic dining. Even if you don't ordinarily relish a flowery wine at dinner, try one with a picnic.

A few basic tips: white wines and rosé should be chilled an hour or so in the refrigerator, except for Sauternes, Barsac, and Champagne, which are served ice-cold and require a couple of hours chilling. Keep your white wines cold en route to the picnic in a cooler — and chill the wine glasses, please! Red wines are served at cellar or cool room temperature, but if it's a very hot day, cool them for half an hour in the cooler. Uncork red wines at least half an hour before serving to let the wine "breathe." This may sound esoteric but it releases the bouquet.

Whatever your wine, give it the thought and attention it deserves.

French Wines

WHITE BURGUNDIES

Chablis — a dry, but soft wine, the most popular of the white Burgundies.

Meursault — one of the great white Burgundies made exclusively from the Pinot Chardonnay grape.

Pouilly-Fuissé — another of the celebrated white Burgundies. Superb!

WHITE BORDEAUX WINES

Graves — medium-dry, delightfully mellow.

Barsac — a fragrant, beautiful wine that varies from medium-sweet to sweet.

Sauternes — sweet, soft, well-rounded. Usually served as a dessert wine, but on a picnic it's delightful with fish. Most famous of the Sauternes is Château d'Yquem.

LOIRE VALLEY WHITE WINES

Muscadet — a very pale, dry white wine that is an excellent accompaniment to shellfish.

Pouilly-Fumé — dry, lovely wine from Sauvignon grapes.

Vouvray — a soft, fruity, pleasant wine. You can also buy sparkling Vouvray.

Sancerre — full-flavored, fruity, one of the better Loire Valley wines.

RED BORDEAUX WINES

St. Julien — fine claret wines from the township of that name in the Médoc district of Bordeaux.

St. Émilion — wines from another district of Bordeaux noted for superior clarets.

Pauillac — great clarets from the Médoc commune of that name.

RED BURGUNDY WINES

Beaune — light-bodied, excellent red wines from the Burgundian village of this name. Beaune Burgundies are singularly light and appropriate for picnics.

SOUTH OF BURGUNDY WINES

Beaujolais —one of the most popular wines, light, fresh, adaptable to most menus. Most famous of the Beaujolais wines are **Moulin-à-Vent, Brouilly, St. Amour,** and **Chenas.**

LOIRE VALLEY RED WINES

Bourgueil — light red wine, pleasant.
Chinon — light wine resembling a Bordeaux.

ROSÉ WINES

Tavel — considered the best rosé in France. It varies from medium-dry to dry.

Anjou Rosé — an excellent mellow rosé from the Anjou region.

German Wines

All the great German wines are white. If you want a red wine, you'll have to look to another country.

Schloss Johannisberger — one of the great German Rhine wines. Others are **Rüdesheimer**, **Geisenheimer**, **Hochheimer**, and **Schloss Vollrads**. All are from Riesling grapes.

Liebfraumilch — a soft, rounded wine from the district of Rheinhessen. Others are **Niersteiner**, **Bodenheimer**, and **Dienheimer**. These are from Sylvaner grapes.

Scharzhofberger — a magnificent, very dry, and flavorful wine from the Saar.

Moselle — fragrant, slightly sweet, full-flavored, and blossomy wines. Best examples are: **Wehlener, Graacher, Zeltinger**, **Bernkasteler**, and **Piesporter Goldtröpfchen**. A popular and good Moselle is **Zeller Schwarze Katz**, but it does not compare in quality to the others.

Italian Wines

WHITE WINES

Orvieto — a memorable, delicate wine; varies from slightly sweet to dry.

Soave — our favorite Italian wine, light, dry, with a beautiful bouquet.

Frascati — full-bodied, dry; quality varies from excellent to poor, but worth investigating.

LIGHT-BODIED RED WINES

Bardolino — light, fresh, fruity wine from Lake Garda. Special!

Valpolicella — another light, fruity, wonderful wine from the north of Italy, in this case from Verona.

Caruso Red — light, dry, and delicate — from the vineyards of Signor Caruso near Ravello on the Southern Italian Riviera.

Caruso Rosé — a beautiful rosé from the same vineyards.

Grignolino — a good, reliable dry table wine from Piedmont.

Valtellina — a group including some of the best wines in Italy. All are from Lombardy. We like the **Inferno** best. Others are **Sassella**, **Grumello**, and **Grigioni**.

California Wines

WHITE WINES

Dry Sauterne — from very dry to slightly mellow, straw-colored, soft.

Haut Sauterne — medium-sweet.

Chablis — dry, delicate white burgundy-type.

Traminer, Gewürztraminer — from an Alsatian grape; fine, fruity flavor.

Johannisberg Riesling — fruity, tart, and rich.

Grey Riesling — soft, light-bodied, fruity.

Emerald Riesling — from a grape variety developed in California; slightly mellow, fruity.

Moselle — flowery, slightly sweet.

Rhine wine — pale and dry.

Pinot Chardonnay — fullest-bodied of the white burgundy-type wines. Special!

Folle Blanche — dry, refreshing wine.

Sauvignon Blanc — a great medium-dry wine.

Pinot Blanc — a white burgundy-type.

Chenin Blanc — medium-dry, fruity, light.

Sylvaner — a good, sprightly white wine from a grape originally developed in Alsace and Germany.

Semillon — a quality white wine varying from sweet to dry.

ROSÉ WINES

Grenache Rosé — medium-dry, pink, fruity, and fresh.

Grignolino Rosé — a distinctive, slightly sweet, fruity wine with a true bouquet.

Vin Rosé — fruity, light, pink, mellow.

RED WINES

Cabernet Sauvignon — most elegant of California red wines; dry, with a distinctive, classic bouquet.

Claret — light, dry bordeaux-type wine.

Beaujolais — light, fresh, delicate red wine of Beaujolais type.

Gamay — a blend principally from the same grape that produces French Beaujolais.

Pinot Noir — light to heavy-bodied; soft, smooth, dry.

Zinfandel — dry, fruity, usually light to medium-bodied.

CALIFORNIA CHAMPAGNES

There are many outstanding California champagnes to choose from, such as **Almadén** or **Korbel**. Our taste preference is for a dry champagne usually labeled **brut** or natural.

New York State Wines

WHITE WINES

Riesling — dry, fresh, one of the most popular New York State wines.

Rhine — Rhine-wine type.

Chablis — dry, light with a somewhat fruity flavor.

Sauterne — dry and fairly tart.

Haut Sauterne — medium-sweet.

Moore's Diamond — spicy, aromatic, and dry.

Delaware — Rhine-wine type; clean, fresh, and fruity with a spicy bouquet.

Dutchess — dry, light, and slightly tart.

Diana — Rhine-wine type; dry, clean, and fairly tart.

RED WINES

Claret — bordeaux-type wine; medium-bodied, soft, and fruity.

NEW YORK STATE CHAMPAGNES

Gold Seal
Great Western

May We Suggest

The following are suggestions for specific wines to serve with those dishes in the book which inspire a good wine. Actually wine is wonderful with anything, including hot dogs, if you love it!

DISH	WINES
Steak au Poivre	California Gamay, or St. Julien
Côte d'Azur Seafood Casserole	California Moselle, or Muscadet
Vitello Tonnato	California Chablis, or Soave
Beef Vinaigrette	California Cabernet or Bardolino
Cold Chicken Vinaigrette	California Traminer, or Liebfraumilch
Stuffed Game Hens	California Gamay, or Beaujolais
Indonesian Pork Saté	California Beaujolais, or Bourgueil
Roast Filet of Beef	California Cabernet Sauvignon, or St. Émilion
Cold Scotch Salmon	New York State Diana, or Scharzhofberger
Meatloaf in Pastry Crust	California Zinfandel, or Caruso Red
Cold Chicken Newport	California Chenin Blanc, or Orvieto
Pizza à la Romana	California Cabernet Sauvignon, or Valpolicella
Salade Niçoise	California Grenache Rosé, or Tavel
White Veal Stew	New York State Riesling, or Schloss Johannisberger
Cold Roast Pork Regina	California Grignolino Rosé, or Caruso Rosé
Cold Sirloin Del Mar	California Pinot Noir, or Beaune
Chicken and Wild Rice Casserole	California Sauvignon Blanc, or Moselle
Cold Shrimp in Pastry Shell	New York State Delaware, or Pouilly-Fuissé
Spaghetti with Wine Sauce	California Cabernet Sauvignon, or Inferno

High Sierra Trout	California Dry Sauterne, or Sancerre
Butterfly Leg of Lamb	New York State Claret, or Bourgueil
Barbecued Lime Chicken	California Dry Semillon, or Vouvray
His Fish	California Folle Blanche, or Orvieto
Charcoal-Broiled Shrimp	California Grey Riesling, or Schloss Johannisberger

CHAPTER X

Picnic Cues

Picnics don't happen, they're staged, like any good road show. When the curtain goes up on *this* production, cold dishes must be cold, hot dishes hot. Every course enters on cue, ready to be served without confusion.

When you consider the number of props that a picnic entails, it's truly a job for a stage manager—or a woman. The smallest details, when overlooked, balloon into major crises. For want of a toothpick the hors d'oeuvres were spoiled, for want of the salt the meat was ruined, for want of a bottle opener the picnic was lost!

Don't trust to memory: plot your picnic on paper. Make a check list of **everything** you're going to bring — and everybody. Try not to forget a guest; this can happen, especially if guests are going in several car pools.

Today there is an intriguing assortment of picnic paraphernalia to facilitate gracious dining even in the wilderness. Insulated containers keep foods as cold, hot, or crisp as you want for hours. Ice is no longer a problem with the spacious ice chests and coolers. There are also chemical refrigerants that afford day-long refrigeration. Light-weight folding grills can be put down anywhere for easy barbecuing. Elegant new plastic glasses have replaced the soggy paper cup, and plastic plates and new regular-size plastic cutlery offer the utmost in convenient dining. Portable folding picnic tables and chairs have moved the movable feast off the ground and away from the ants. At the end of this section there is a list of some of the newest and most useful picnic accessories.

Whatever your equipment, fancy or makeshift, one indispensable item wraps up every good picnic: aluminum foil. You can't move without it. Foil adapts to more uses than most people realize. Aside from keeping foods fresh and protected, it is a remarkable insulator. Double-wrap foil around a hot casserole right from the oven, wrap again in newspaper, and the casserole stays appetizingly hot for hours. The reverse is true for foods cold from the refrigerator. Wrap them in foil and, in this case, wet newspaper, and you insulate the chill—even the shiver. Aluminum-foil wrapping also retards ice cubes from melting in the cooler. Explore the practical uses of foil in barbecuing; line your brazier or grill with it and you'll get the benefit of reflected heat. Use it for steaming vegetables on top of the grill or for foil-cooked meats. Shape it into cups to hold basting sauces.

For wrapping, the 12-inch, heavy-duty foil is most serviceable. Place the food or container on the foil a bit off center. Bring the foil up over the food so the edges meet. Fold all the edges in toward the food two or three times in ½-inch folds to seal securely. It is a good idea to line your picnic baskets with foil, especially if you're having a beach picnic. Sand ruins more picnics than ants.

While we're on wrapping, here are three other pointers:
  (1) Tape the lids of all containers that don't have secure screw-top caps. Picnics get a lot of joggling, and nothing provokes more tears than spilt milk— unless it's spilt juleps.

(2) Label every package clearly so there won't be any confusion on arrival of what you did with the oyster forks or what package has the Wild Boar Cutlets.

(3) Package your picnic in the sequence in which it will unfold. The last thing in the hamper should be the first thing to be served. Pack all the baskets and equipment in the car the same way, especially if you are giving a tailgate picnic, so you can reach first things first.

The simple sandwich or snack picnic that unwraps on the beach, grandstand, or out of a knapsack is best packaged in individual servings like a box lunch. Use plastic containers and forks for salads or side dishes—and put in those miniature salt and pepper shakers you can get in grocery stores. A half-gallon or gallon thermos for hot or cold soups or beverages can be carried separately, as can insulated drinking mugs. Like foil, ice is an integral part of every picnic, hot or cold, simple or elaborate. It keeps chilled foods from spoiling on a summer day. You have to be especially careful of dishes with mayonnaise or creamy sauces. Refrigeration is easy and accessible with the variety of styrene-foam chests, coolers, and insulated containers on the market. Even if you don't have a regular ice chest, it's easy to devise one with an ordinary pail. Collect a load of ice cubes in advance or buy them in a vending machine. Put the ice in plastic bags. Line the bottom of the pail with foil, then with damp newspapers, and put the plastic bags on top. Cover with foil again. Another smart way to conserve ice is to wrap several small pieces of dry ice inside a hand towel and place on top of the ice cubes in your cooler. Or fill quart-sized plastic detergent bottles almost full of water; close tightly and store in the freezer compartment. These bottles turn into effective, long-lasting chilling agents to supplement the ice.

In addition to ice and dry ice, there is an amazingly efficient gel refrigerant on the market that keeps things icy cold all day. Make a note for your sportsman's lunchbox. It's perfect for chilling his beer or Coke and for keeping the sandwiches fresh. This refrigerant is also great for knapsack picnics.

All right, the food is wrapped and packed, you've got more ice cubes than General Electric, and you're ready to go! But are you? We hope you'll write down on that check list these most frequently forgotten and essential items:

Drinking water. Don't count on the little babbling brook or water fountain. They're never there.

Can opener and bottle opener. It's better to forget a guest than to forget the bottle opener.

Cutting knife and paring knife. There's always something to be sliced or pared on a picnic, no matter how thoroughly you've done your homework. Bring Woolworth knives — if you lose them, so what?

Bread board. Another essential, which can be pressed into service for everything from a tray for serving drinks to a steak platter. You can also use it as a bread board.

Extra napkins. Don't be stingy with the napkins. Bring a whole box — picnics are napkin-gobblers.

Paper towels. Again, bring a whole roll. You'll be glad when it's clean-up time.

Two large paper bags or cardboard cartons. Clean-ups are much easier if you put all your burnable trash in one bag or box, and your bottles and cans in another. Unless you can find a trash can in paradise, you'll have to take the bottles and cans home.

Pail for carrying water. You may never use it, but chances are you will, either for cleaning up or putting out the barbecue fire. The pail can go to the picnic full of ice.

Wash 'n Dry or similar cleansing washcloths. Unless you're bringing your cut-crystal finger bowls, we'd advise you to take these handy paper "wipes," which are saturated with cleansing lotion. Take a packet for each guest. Finger food is fun, but oh those sticky fingers!

Spray can of insect repellent. A good picnic brings out the insect population in force. Be prepared.

Once you have the show on the road, all that remains is to move the feast from car to picnic site. This is a real chore if your picnic is unfolding some distance from the car—on the beach or by some secluded stream. However, there are simple solutions to the lifting problem:

(1) Pack your picnic in large baskets or hampers with handles that can be strung on a long bamboo pole. The pole is carried by a man at each end—an ancient but efficient means of transportation.

(2) Tote your picnic on a light-weight folding cot. It's not only easy to carry over rough terrain, but makes a handy picnic table when it's set up.

We'd like to conclude with a word about picnic sites. How do you find an untrampled paradise today? State parks and beaches are often crowded, especially in season. Dining by the side of the highway is just as private and relaxing as it sounds. Main roads, even in California, are fenced. Idyllic picnic sites are increasingly difficult to find but not impossible. It takes some hill-and-vale venturing away from the highways. My husband and I have discovered the choicest picnic havens by just browsing along the back roads (the unpaved ones seem to produce the best results). If you inquire, farmers will often let you encamp on their land for a small fee.

Whatever the effort required, there's nothing more joyous or human than a picnic. It's more than a meal, it's a recreation, and one of the few that a family can enjoy together for relatively little expense.

Picnic Accessories

The following is a round-up of the latest in picnic ware; also some standard items to put in the hamper. You'll find these accessories at import stores, gift shops, hardware and department stores, sporting-goods stores, and gourmet grocery stores.

Large stack carrier basket. From Taiwan; has four compartments of different depths. Ideal picnic carrier.

Assorted imported picnic baskets. Wicker and woven bamboo. The least expensive are found in Mexican and Japanese stores.

Fitted Swedish and English picnic baskets. Contain service for 4 or 8. Completely equipped—cutlery, dishes, vacuum bottles, etc.

Mexican hemp bags. Brightly colored and practical for toting extras.

Styrene-foam chests. Keep ice all day or hot foods hot for at least 4 or 5 hours. Light-weight, inexpensive, available in various sizes.

Insulated carrying bags. Some are equipped with two insulated, water-proof containers for carrying hot or cold foods.

Half-gallon insulated jugs. Keep hot drinks or soups up to 8 hours, cold liquids for 36 hours. Available with wide mouths for easy pouring. For hot and cold beverages, there are twin half-gallon jugs packaged in a handy traveling case.

Stainless steel vacuum bottles and stainless steel food jars. Available in quart or pint size; provide day-long thermal protection.

Insulated casserole. Has insulated lid, liner to cook in. Keeps foods hot or cold for at least 4 hours.

Re-usable gel refrigerant. Easily frozen. Comes in flexible containers. An indispensible item for chilling foods and to use as an ice supplement.

Japanese soy tub. Doubles as a great ice bucket to chill beverages. Has convenient rope handles.

Aluminum five-layer stack pail. Handles clip the pans tightly together; pail carries five different foods in one unit. When unclipped, pans double as serving dishes. A specialty of Japanese stores.

Outing Kit. Ideal for a sportsman's lunchbox. Waterproof case is equipped with large food box and two quart-size vacuum bottles, one with standard neck and one with wide mouth.

Completely collapsible plastic jug. Just the thing for carrying cold liquids such as drinking water. Unbreakable.

Plastic tubes to carry condiments. Tubes fill from the bottom, safely transport mustard, catsup, etc.

Plastic basin for clean-ups. Folds flat when empty.

Cold Keg Can Popper-Upper. A slim, easy-to-carry cylinder that keeps 6 cans of beer or soda ice-cold for hours. One can pops up at a time.

Swiss Army Knife. Has two blades, nail file, screwdriver, cap lifter, can opener, reamer, double-cut saw, scissors, toothpick — and tweezers. You'd be surprised how many of these tools you use on a picnic.

Aluminum folding stool with drill seat. Inexpensive.

Wicker folding chairs. Fold and nest for easy storing.

Folding wicker beach rest. Has compartment underneath for carrying picnic foods and drinks.

Folding aluminum table 32 by 74 (30 inches high). Folds compactly; has plastic handles for easy carrying.

Slatted-top table, 3 feet square. Rolls up to make a 7 by 36-inch cylinder for easy carrying. Has folding legs.

Gaily decorated vinyl tablecloths. Easily sponged; provide an elegant table covering.

Roll of Japanese matting. Most useful as a table covering or to sit on; comes in 3 by 6-foot length. Available in Oriental import stores.

Individual, colorful cardboard tables. Can also be used as seats. Can be set up in seconds. Good for tailgate picnics.

Disposable plastic glasses. Remarkably attractive and available in various sizes and shapes. Can be used many times.

Thermo steins, old-fashioneds, mugs, and tumblers. Double-wall insulation. Shatterproof.

Regular-size plastic cutlery. The latest innovation for picnic dining.

Plastic or Melmac dinner plates. Also available in variety stores or hardware stores. Reasonable.

Wicker bases for paper plates and bowls. Hold and support plates; available in 10-inch size.

Trays with disposable liners. Perfect for picnics afloat. Trays are 10½ inches long and can be used with disposable water-and-grease-resistant liners.

Clam-lobster cooker. Large, colorfully decorated, baked blue enamel. Has faucet in the bottom to draw off juices. Capacity either 20 or 38 quarts.

Folding grill. Simple cooking units that pack compactly for easy transporting.

French stove with butane tank. Small, light; operates on replaceable cartridges. Can be used where open fires are restricted.

Hibachi. Japanese grill, ideal for picnic barbecuing. Inexpensive.

Camp stove and oven. For camper cookery when camper is not equipped with a stove. This one operates on bottled fuel and affords regular cooking and baking.

Folding Paper Flame Grill. Broils steaks in 6 minutes using four sheets of newspaper as fuel. No other fuel is necessary. Sets up in seconds, folds flat to about 1 foot square, fits under a car seat.

Vertibroil. An excellent grill that broils meat vertically. Meats retain juices while fat drips into a tray, thus preventing flare-ups.

Jumbo skillet. Perfect for fish fries. Skillet is 20 inches wide with a 27-inch handle. Made of aluminum.

Disposable fry pans. Re-usable foil fry pans with stay-cool handles. Great for camper breakfasts.

Cook 'n Stir. A compact unit that does everything — cooks, blends, stirs, and operates on a thermostatic control. It looks like a blender with a food container capacity of 1½ quarts. Ideal for hot motel breakfasts.

Quick-boil immersion heater. An electric unit that heats water, soups, etc., in a matter of minutes. Also recommended for motel breakfasts.

Hot Plate. An indispensable portable stove that works on electricity. Perfect for room picnics. Available in single or double units. Inexpensive.

Popcorn popper. Doubles as an ideal cooking or warming pot for quick motel breakfasts.

A Note on Preserving Perishables

We'd like to add a footnote emphasizing the importance of safe-guarding perishable foods—not only en route but at home. Often picnics must be kept for hours or sometimes overnight before you depart, and are vulnerable to spoilage, especially in hot weather. The perfect summer's day that makes a picnic can also melt it. Almost all foods perish or wilt without protection—right down to the seemingly indestructible pickle. Some foods are more vulnerable than others, of course. Mayonnaise and hamburger spoil rapidly when not refrigerated, while the sturdy hard-cooked egg keeps its cool for hours off the ice. To be absolutely safe, it's a wise policy to keep *all* picnic foods refrigerated from the moment you've prepared them. This includes fried chicken or hot casseroles if you plan to keep them for even an hour before departure. They can easily be re-heated and properly insulated just before you leave. Four hours out of the refrigerator is the maximum holding time for safety.

As we've already mentioned, aluminum foil is indispensable in transporting a picnic; it's also essential in keeping it airtight and fresh in the refrigerator. (Air, as well as heat, dries out and ruins foods.) There are varieties of good plastic wraps that offer the same protection, as well as plastic sandwich bags that are the greatest thing that has happened to sandwiches since peanut butter. Plastic refrigerator containers also keep a picnic airtight and preserve even fruit salad without discoloration. They're good travelers, too.

Here are some basic rules to follow in safeguarding perishables:

The following foods must be kept thoroughly chilled at all times: mayonnaise, any ground meats including sausage, seafood, pork, custards, milk, cream, or anything with creamy fillings. Stuffed foods should never travel very far.

Carry salad dressing and washed and dried salad greens in separate containers to the picnic and combine just before serving. This also applies to sauces.

Butter all sandwiches whatever the filling. Butter insulates the bread and protects it from getting soggy. Go lightly on the mayonnaise in making sandwich fillings, and try and avoid "damp" ingredients such as lettuce and tomatoes, especially unless you toast the bread. Wrap sandwiches individually in plastic bags rather than in stacks, to insure freshness.

Frozen juices or other frozen foods should not be defrosted before departure. Wrap in foil and keep cold until ready to use.

Season and prepare hamburger patties at home so they're ready for the grill. The less handling of ground meat in the sun, the better.

Cakes fare better than creamy pies at picnics. To protect cake frosting, stick several toothpicks on top of cake before wrapping tightly in foil.

Remove food from ice chests as needed; don't unpack your entire picnic at once and leave it out in the sun.

Aside from the danger of food poisoning, wilted foods are unappetizing and unattractive. Make sure that all your picnic ingredients are *fresh* from the market; never use meats and vegetables that have been sitting around in the refrigerator for days.

Index